Not THE BODYGUARD'S *Baby*

Other Books By Lorin Grace

American Homespun Series
Waking Lucy
Remembering Anna
Reforming Elizabeth
Healing Sarah

Artists & Billionaires
Mending Fences
Mending Christmas
Mending Walls
Mending Images
Mending Words
Mending Hearts

Hastings Security
Not the Bodyguard's Widow
Not the Bodyguard's Boss
Not the Bodyguard's Princess
Not the Bodyguard's Bride

The Miscellaneous Royalty
Miss Guided
Miss Oriented

Not THE BODYGUARD'S *Baby*

LORIN GRACE

Cover Design © 2019 Evan Frederickson
Photos © iStock

Formatting by LJP Creative
Edits by Eschler Editing

Published by Currant Creek Press
North Logan, Utah

First edition: March 2019
ISBN: 978-1-970148-02-2

to Julie

EVERY AUTHOR NEEDS A FAN

— Office. NOW!!

Adam didn't bother returning the text from Hastings Security's new secretary as he wove through the parking garage. By the time he answered, he could be in the office. Since she hadn't used any of the alert codes, texting her back could prove fatal. Chunks of ice and snow brought in by the various vehicles had created puddles that awaited unsuspecting business men. He dodged the water traps, attempting to keep his pants clean. Tuesdays were suit days, and the new dark-gray one had replaced the one he'd ruined two weeks ago taking down a pepper-spray-wielding threat. More puddles awaited on the sidewalk between the garage and Ogilvie Tower. After a lifetime in Chicago, he knew better than to trust his good shoes to the weather.

A few people sat in the lobby sipping from steaming cups and trading gossip. Others crowded the hallway in front of the elevator bays with the intent of getting to their desks in the dozens of businesses housed in the tower. Adam bypassed the elevator for the stairs, the fastest route to the third floor.

Sprinting up the empty stairway, he double-checked his holster. No telling what awaited him in the office. Elle's lack of emergency code troubled him—although she'd only been training for a week and might not remember them. At the door to the third floor, he paused, listening for anything out of the ordinary as he noiselessly opened the door.

A muffled cry came from the west side of the building where the Hastings Security office resided. The cry didn't sound like an adult's. Adam used the dome mirror across from the elevator to look at the reception desk through the open doorway.

No one sat at the desk.

Adam unholstered his gun and inched down the hallway in search of danger. Closer to the doorway, he could see that Elle stood in the hallway, her back to the main door, swaying back and forth in time to a song only she could hear. He sighed. Part of her duty included never leaving the desk unmanned.

The angle of the hallway offered a tactical disadvantage to someone entering the office, as it had been designed, and Adam watched for a moment to determine the threat. Elle conversed with someone beyond his view yet remained calm. Friend or foe he couldn't tell from this angle. She continued swaying and bouncing. Adam slipped into the office knowing he would trigger the pressure pad under the carpet, lighting a display behind the reception desk and back in the dispatch area. He wondered if Elle had managed to push the alert button before she got up. If so, his brothers should be here soon. Keeping close to the wall, he craned his neck to get a better view down the hallway.

Just beyond Elle stood a man with cropped gray hair, arms crossed, brow furrowed and disapproving. Jethro Hastings. Adam holstered his gun. The last time he had seen that look on his father's face was fifteen years ago, when he was a sophomore at the university and had come home to help his brothers sabotage his sister's prom date. Poor Elle. He liked the new secretary and hoped whatever she had done to cause his father's ire, she wouldn't lose her job.

Jethro Hastings jerked his chin toward Adam, and as Elle spun around, a small tiny wail filled the air. She patted a bundle in her arms. No wonder his father was glaring. Babies didn't belong in the office.

"Where did the baby come from?"

Jethro Hastings stepped around the receptionist. "I was about to ask you the same thing. She is yours."

"Me? I don't have a baby!" He hadn't even had a girlfriend the past year.

"According to the letter tucked in the car seat, you do." He handed Adam a folded paper.

Adam,

Our daughter's name is Harmony. She is six weeks old. I'm not in a good place.

I need you to keep her safe for a while.

September

After five years as the singer's head of security, he would recognize her rounded scrawl anywhere. Six weeks. That meant the baby had been born the first week of January, so nine months before…Why bother calculating? He'd kissed September once, and that had been a year ago last December. He had never been the type for one-night stands or to sleep around. No way, no how could he be the child's father.

Jethro turned to Elle and the crying baby, and for a moment, his face softened. "Give her to him, and thanks." Jethro returned down the hallway to the office and firmly shut the door.

"She isn't mine." Couldn't be. Impossible. If this was one of his brothers' jokes…Even Andrew was smart enough not to get Dad this upset. He blinked, trying to wake himself up from this nightmare, but nothing changed.

Elle held the baby out to him. "Isn't any of my business. I need to get back to work. I'm not supposed to leave the desk unattended."

Adam tucked the baby into his arm like he would a football. She stopped crying for a moment, then blinked at him. Why would

September leave her child with him? Perhaps she had been in drug rehab like the tabloids claimed. But the sweet woman he remembered...

When the baby cried again and spit up on his suit, Adam hurried back to his office, wondering if this suit would survive the day.

September held the pen over the patient-signature line on the admitting forms. If she didn't sign, she could leave now, go get Harmony, and disappear. Maybe last night wouldn't replay and she could just sing a song and be happy. Things were not that bad. Were they? She closed her eyes and saw her baby's sweet face and signed the first paper.

A woman joined the admitting nurse. "Miss Platt, I'm Maria, one of the social workers assigned to the behavioral-health unit. We are unclear on part of your story. Where is your baby now?"

"She is safe. I left her at Adam's office with plenty of diapers and formula. I tried to pump, but I couldn't get the bottle to fill up. I know—" September burst into tears. If only the tears and sadness would leave. She'd thought she would be happy when the baby arrived. At first she had been, but then, one day, Harmony had stopped sleeping and cried for hours. And September had started thinking the unthinkable. The nurse passed over a new box of tissues.

"So where is your husband's office?"

"I'm not married. Adam works at Hastings Security, downtown." September pulled Adam's card from her wallet.

The social worker read the card before answering. "When was the last time you spoke to Mr. Adam?"

Over a year, but she couldn't tell her that, so she shrugged. "A while ago."

"Are you sure he will take care of your child?"

"I haven't been too sure of anything these past few hours. Other than that I needed to get help and make sure Harmony was in the safest place I could find. No place is safer than with Adam." September blew her nose and tucked the used tissue in her pocket. She didn't need some half-crazed fan trying to sell it online. But with no makeup and her hair in a messy bun, she was sure no one would recognize her, especially with the baby weight she now carried. Her manager would be furious if she knew where September was. Shyla Manning would find a suitable facility in some discreet location, far from prying eyes, but her ob-gyn had been clear during their visit yesterday. Sometimes new mothers needed in-house help to deal with postpartum depression, or PPD. For some, it was a matter of either getting help or becoming a tragic news story. After the few insane moments she'd experienced early this morning, she'd held on to enough clarity to follow the doctor's orders, knowing something was very wrong with her.

"I've heard of Hastings Security. They are bodyguards to some of Chicago's most elite. But they aren't babysitters." The social worker took the seat next to September.

"I've known them most of my life. Mrs. Hastings loves children. She'll help Adam." She wiped her eyes again, glad she hadn't worn makeup for days. The dripping-mascara look was never as glamorous as on screen when overseen by a makeup artist.

"Ms. Platt, I am confused. The card you handed me says 'Mr. Adam.' You keep calling him Adam."

"His real name is Adam Hastings. With four brothers working for their father, it gets confusing, so they go by their first names. Mr. Adam, Mr. Alan, Mr. Alex, and Mr. Andrew. Only their sister Abbie used their last name." Why were random facts like these so clear when ten minutes ago she couldn't tell the intake nurse her last meal? If her mom were still alive, she would have been as kind as Melanie Hastings. Adam's mother was the type September wished she could be. Mrs. Hastings would be the perfect surrogate grandmother for Harmony, and she would teach Adam what to do. The thought of Melanie, even more than Adam, had been what prompted her to turn off the car inside the locked garage of her suburban Chicago house and not take her life and the life of her newborn. If Mrs. Hastings could raise her own five children, September could at least be strong enough to call her ob-gyn and admit things were well past spinning out of control.

The social worker tapped the business card on the desk. "I will call in a welfare check on the baby while they finish admitting you. We want both you and your daughter to be safe."

Did the police do the welfare checks? September didn't dare ask out loud. Jethro Hastings would not be happy to have the police snooping around his office. Had she done the right thing? Wouldn't it have been easier to let the car keep running until she never needed to cry again?

September took another tissue from the box and wiped away the tears as she signed yet another form.

"ABBIE, STOP LAUGHING OR I'LL end the video call." Adam used a second baby wipe to try to clean the white ooze from the front of his suit coat. His sister covered her mouth but kept laughing. "I need help, and with Mom out of town, I don't know where else to turn. September left her baby here, and I'm clueless."

"Why not call September's manager or Child Services?"

How could he explain? Most of the music star's life consisted of an illusion created by her manager. If September hadn't left the baby with Shyla, he would respect that. The existence of the baby was evidence enough to call in to doubt the "official" story that September had checked into rehab six months ago. The baby looked healthy—a fact he would double-check later. He'd assumed an addict's baby would be scrawny. "Because September left her with me, and I have to think she had a reason." Or maybe he just hoped she did. The vague note needed clarification. What did she mean by a "bad place?" After all those years of avoiding the dark side of stardom, had she succumbed to one of the many men who'd dated her with less-than-honorable motives? A rebound relationship to replace him? September wasn't the first woman he had fallen hard for in his thirty-five years. But she'd been the last. No matter how unsuitable their relationship had been, he wished for a do-over.

"How am I supposed to help you?" Abbie twisted the end of her ponytail.

"You are going to be a mom in five months. You should know this stuff. How do I change a diaper?" Information he needed now.

Abbie frowned. "Wow, that sounded almost as sexist as those guys who didn't believe I could be a bodyguard."

Adam groaned and reached for another baby wipe. Offending his four-month-pregnant sister was not a good move, even if she couldn't take him down in a sparring match at the moment. "Abs, that isn't what I meant. You have been reading books and hanging out with your friend and her baby and even interviewing some helpers for after the triplets are born."

"Yes, but I have been reading about dealing with triplets, and the help I have been interviewing is because I'm not an octopus. I can't hold three bottles at once, and even with both of our mothers' help . . . but that is my problem. You've been around children before. Haven't you helped with the Crawford's detail since Joy was born?"

"I've spent almost as much time as Alex has on the Crawford's security, but that doesn't mean I know how to change a diaper. I don't think I've seen anyone change a diaper since Mom changed Andrew's over twenty-five years ago."

"There has to be someone in the office who can help. Marco is a father—oh, but he is out this week for Valentine's Day, isn't he? Elle has lots of nieces and nephews. Isn't she working today?"

"Elle's job doesn't include babysitting, and I'm not crossing Dad to ask her. It's my problem to solve." Avoiding the inevitable follow-up conversation with his dad sat at the top of his to-do list, right after the diaper. Adam hadn't ever told his father, or anyone else, the complete story of why he'd quit the job overseeing September's music-tour security, allowing a competing firm to pick up the lucrative project.

Abbie crossed her arms. "She is a baby, not a problem."

"But she isn't my baby, and that is a problem."

"Changing a diaper isn't difficult. Make sure you have a clean diaper ready. Put her on a changing pad if you can find one. It may be the same material as the diaper bag but white and waterproof on one side. Wipe front to back, and don't let her fall. In fact, you may want to change her on the floor so you don't have to worry about that. How old is she?"

"According to the note, about six weeks. But who knows?"

Abbie leaned closer to her camera. "You told me you crossed the line with September when you warned me about my last job and getting too emotionally involved with Preston. What exactly did you mean by 'crossing the line'?"

Falling in love. And not that Abbie had listened to him. His sister had ignored his advice and married her client anyway. At least she got a happy ending.

"I kissed September. That's all. I knew I couldn't keep my objectivity around her and that she wouldn't be safe, so I quit the next day." Or was fired. The words she'd said when he apologized for kissing her could be taken that way. September probably had a different take on that moment, which made giving him the baby even more confusing. "I haven't even texted her in the past eleven months—" Harmony's cry saved him from needing to say more. An unpleasant oder wafted through the room. "Hey, sis, I gotta go. Smells like I need to change a diaper."

"Good luck." The screen went black.

Adam held the baby with one arm and dug through the diaper bag with the other, pulling out a fresh diaper and a changing pad. He took his sister's advice and knelt on the floor. "Okay, little one. How hard can this be?"

Adam pulled the baby's pink leggings down to her ankles to discover the shirt was held in place by a row of snaps. Underneath that, he found an undershirt held in place by another row of snaps. "They didn't design this for a fast removal, did they?"

The baby blinked up at him.

Adam released the fasteners on either side of the diaper and tried to slip it off, but the puffy disposable wouldn't fit through her legs. Adam removed the baby's little pink booties and leggings and tried again to remove the dirty diaper. Yuck. Was that color of orange even natural? Using seven baby wipes, he tried to follow his sister's instructions. Someone tapped on his office door.

"Enter." Adam turned to look at the door. At the same time, the baby passed more gas than a helium balloon along with more of the orange goop. Abbie had neglected to warn him that babies could launch projectiles from both ends, at least he had been prepared for the spit up. Perhaps at halfway through her pregnancy, she hadn't learned yet.

Elle covered her mouth to stop a laugh. The young police officer next to her didn't seem amused, but the older female officer attempted to hide a smile. She probably had more experience than he did in the child-changing category.

Something dripped down Adam's cheek. Orange goop speckled his new shirt.

The baby made a satisfied cooing sound.

Elle dropped to her knees next to Adam, took a couple of wipes, and handed the box to Adam. "Let me finish this. Next time you try to change a diaper, be at the side of the baby. The officer needs to speak with you. I suggest you go wash up first."

The officer stepped back into the hallway next to his partner, a female in her midthirties who didn't even try to hide her smile now as Adam advanced. "If you will give me a minute, I'll be right back."

"Take all the time you need." Laughter tinged the female officer's voice.

The bathroom mirror told Adam what he already suspected. He needed a change of clothes. He stripped to the waist and started washing the best he could over the sink. The door behind him swung open to reveal his brother Andrew holding a new shirt, still in its plastic bag. "Elle, said you might need this. You sure you don't want to go down to the workout room and use the shower?"

Adam shook his head and took the shirt. The security teams used navy polos with the word *security* emblazoned on the backs with the silver Hastings shield on the right sleeve for jobs where the appearance of being present provided a deterrent. At least the shirt was clean. Adam glanced at his watch. Not even 10:00 a.m. He hoped there were more shirts where this one came from. He wrapped his dirty blue dress shirt in the plastic bag and tossed it in the trash, along with the tie. Even if he could clean them, he doubted he would ever wear either again. Memories didn't clean out in the laundry.

The officers were waiting in his office. The baby carrier sat empty on the floor. Adam held up a finger and backed out the door. He found Elle rocking the baby in the break room. She put her finger to her lips as he approached, and waved him away.

Adam returned to his office. "Sorry to keep you waiting. How can I help you?"

The female officer stood. "I think we have seen everything we need to see. We came to do a welfare check on Harmony Platt." The officer next to her nodded.

His heart raced. They couldn't take the baby away. "Officers, I assure you I can take care of her. What you saw—"

The female officer stopped him. "You misunderstand me. I am not worried about your diaper-changing skills. You'll learn in time. You didn't get sprayed nearly as badly as my husband the first time he changed our son." She smiled. "When you returned to the room, the first thing you did was look for your daughter—the mark of a good father when he puts the welfare of his child above his own."

The other officer stepped forward. "You had no idea why we were here but chose to ignore us until you knew where your baby was. I've been on many welfare checks where the parents wanted to impress me first. Those are the parents I worry about."

Adam thought about correcting the officer as to his paternal status, but the fact that they were doing a welfare check on September's child raised red flags he didn't want to complicate. He'd rather not need to search for a baby lost in the system. "Thank you, Officers. September was rather vague when she dropped off the baby. Can you tell me where she is?"

The officers looked at each other, then back at him. "You mean she didn't tell you where she went?"

"No, she didn't." *Please don't let her be into drugs—not this soon after a baby.*

"I'm sorry, sir. We are not authorized to give out that information."

"Can you tell me who asked you to do the welfare check?"

The younger officer's eyes narrowed, and the female officer studied Adam before answering. "A social worker contacted us from the facility where the mother has self-admitted and is safe. I am sure someone will be contacting you soon."

The young officer glared at his partner.

"Thank you for telling me. I won't press you for more. Is there anything else you need?"

The female officer offered him her card. "I should be asking you that. I noticed the formula in the diaper bag. I am assuming from the explosive nature of the diaper that up until now your daughter has been breastfed. I wrote the name of a better brand of formula on the back you might want to try if she doesn't like the one you are using. You'll know if she spits up most of the formula that the brand isn't working for her."

Adam took the card. He wouldn't ask how the officer knew September had nursed the baby. Too many pieces weren't fitting together. Mothers who cared about their children didn't abandon them. But abandoned children usually were not well-fed—at least not the ones who made the news. September hadn't done drugs when he knew her. Knowing her manager, the story about September spending the last six months in rehab was a cover-up. But that left the most puzzling question of all—where was September, and what had prompted a welfare check?

The generic-gray hospital-issue scrubs were too long for September and dragged on the floor. Rolling them up was too much work. How did they expect people to not be depressed wearing something so ugly? Couldn't they at least get some cute scrubs like the kind pediatric nurses wore? September followed a woman wearing the same gray outfit into a small room lined with couches. One other woman sat in the room, also dressed in gray. She didn't look up as they came in. Another woman carrying a tablet and dressed in business attire entered the room and closed the door.

"I am Dr. Tamara Brooks. First, let me apologize for the gray clothing. If I had my choice, I would give you different tops. The behavioral-health unit is an integrated facility serving a number of different patients. For this reason, there are no shoelaces or tie strings in your clothing. After tomorrow you should all be moved to the third floor where we've set up a small unit for postpartum treatment. This is a new program still in the pilot stage. For part of each day, your infant will be in the unit with you. This will allow you to nurse and bond with your child while in therapy. If ever you feel overwhelmed, we've got a full staff of caregivers on the floor to help both you and your child."

The woman in the corner raised her hand. "I thought the drugs meant we couldn't breastfeed anymore."

"Several antidepressants don't cross over into the milk and are considered safe for both baby and mother. Your doctors will discuss your medication with you. Every effort is made to help you continue nursing if you wish."

The mention of nursing caused September's milk to let down. She was going to leak any minute.

"There are hospital-grade pumps for you to use. One of the redeeming qualities of your scrub tops is they are roomy enough to pump under and give you some privacy. Due to the cording on the pumps, you will be supervised by either a nurse or a lactation consultant whenever you are pumping. Looks like a couple of you would like to pump now instead of later. How about I rearrange your morning?" Dr. Brooks crossed the room and used the ID card on her lanyard to open the door. She stayed in the doorway as she talked to someone, then returned to the couches. "They'll have the pumps and a lactation specialist down here in a moment. The first time I used a hospital pump, it was a little intimidating."

The doctor was a mom too. September breathed a sigh of relief. Maybe the doctor would understand.

"Five years ago, I sat where you are today. Only five years ago the hospital was mixing the new moms with all the other patients, including men. The PPD ward is a women-only ward. This includes employees, many of whom, like me, have personal experience with postpartum depression. Males, including doctors, are allowed only in the meeting rooms and offices outside the unit."

Someone tapped on the door. Dr. Brooks answered, and a nurse pushed a cart with three pumps into the room.

"I'll be back in half an hour. Don't worry about how much you pump. If it doesn't seem like a full bottle's worth, don't worry. The first few times with a pump can be frustrating."

One of the women laughed nervously.

The nurse provided instructions, and within a few moments, the only sounds in the room came from the machines.

The woman to September's left gasped. "I wish my twins would eat this fast."

"You have twins?" asked the woman on her right.

"They are three months old. And I can't—" The woman took a deep breath. "My name is Leisha. I figure if I can pump in front of you, we may as well be on a first-name basis." Her voice carried a slight twang.

Another woman chimed in. "I'm Madison. My son is ten weeks old, and my other son had his second birthday on Sunday."

September glanced at her hospital band, glad her middle name was the name on it—the name she had asked the hospital to list as her preferred name. "My name is Rayne, and my daughter is six weeks old."

Leisha stared at September for a moment, her large brown eyes narrowing. "You remind me of someone. Have we met before?"

"I don't think so. Where did you grow up?"

"Down in Alabama. No matter how hard I try, I can't get rid of my accent. What about you, Madison?"

"I'm from Lake Forest, so I am pretty much a native."

September recognized the name of the posh suburb. She had looked at homes there before purchasing one in Oak Brook. Before Leisha could ask another question, her pump beeped and the nurse came over. "I believe you are finished." The nurse helped them untangle themselves.

September wondered how long she would be able to keep her identity a secret. She guessed it was only a matter of time before Leisha made the connection.

A FEW MINUTES AFTER THE police left, Elle brought the slumbering baby into Adam's office. "Your father wants to visit with you. He asked that I keep Harmony in here."

"Thanks, Elle. I'll be back in a few." *I hope.* Adam walked down the hallway to his father's office.

Jethro Hastings sat behind his desk in his leather chair. "Shut the door."

Adam complied and sat in front of the desk.

"First off, I believe you. If you say you are not the father, you're not. But that doesn't change what the note says. Since the police didn't leave with the baby, I presume you didn't deny paternity." Jethro raised his brows, waiting for Adam to answer the unasked questions.

"Assuming the child is September's and not part of some weird stunt, she must have been desperate to name me as the father and then leave the baby here. It doesn't make much sense, even if this is one of her manager's stunts. I don't see what the endgame would be. If they want publicity, there are a dozen A-listers she could pin paternity on. I'm a nobody bodyguard. No money or anything."

"There is your sister and her husband." His sister Abbie's marriage into one of the wealthiest families in the United States had taken her from guarding others to being guarded. To the best of Adam's knowledge, they'd received no more threats than any of the others in Chicago's elite.

Adam shook his head. "Why bring them into it? There is no reason for Preston and Abbie to pay to keep this quiet. September is hardly the first star to deliver a child out of wedlock. Could this be something to discredit Hastings Security?"

"Maybe. Do you know who has September's security contract now?"

"After I quit, her manager, Shyla, hired a security firm out of LA. I heard she fired them the week September checked into rehab. I have heard nothing official since."

Jethro leaned forward. "For September being a former client, you're keeping pretty good tabs on her..."

Again, his father hadn't asked a question. This time Adam refused to be baited. He'd lost his heart long before the night he'd lost his head and kissed September. His head might be back on straight, but his heart remained in recovery. The resemblance of the baby to her mother was making him lose his heart all over again. He couldn't help following what September was doing in the news. Every time he surfed social media, he sought out information about her, even after swearing he wouldn't. There had been very little media about September for months now. The only recent news indicated the possibility of a tour in the fall and a pending movie contract.

Jethro frowned. "I don't like this. I wasn't comfortable with the whole rehab thing, either. What job were you heading up?"

"I've been helping Andrew set up security for Ogilvie's and spelling off Alex on the Crawfords. They intertwine the two jobs."

"I'm pulling you off both. Consider the baby a client, since whatever is going on, she is the only innocent party. May as well move in at our house. Your mother will be back tomorrow. Your apartment isn't big enough for the two of you."

"I thought Mom would be out with Grandma another week." Not that he would turn down any help.

"When I called and informed her you were a father, she changed her plans. There is a port-a-crib in Abbie's old room. Your mother has been collecting things at garage sales for years in anticipation of being a grandmother. May as well get some use out of them."

"Who exactly am I guarding the baby against?"

"That is something you will need to figure out. I don't want any PIs on this. We handled September's parents' security before their deaths and September's until last year. I feel I owe them as much privacy as we can give them after two decades of working with them. I will discreetly ask around to find out who she currently employs. It will be helpful if we can at least figure out where she is living, as I assume it isn't some Puget Sound detox center as her website claims." Jethro stood and came around the desk. "Keep me in the loop. I still think of September as family. I'll have Elle screen and forward your calls to your cell."

"Thanks, I'll see you later." Adam returned to his office. Elle sat in his desk chair with the baby.

"I'm going to my parents' house with her. Was there anything besides the diaper bag and the car seat?" Adam gathered up the items he'd pulled out of the bag earlier.

"Only the letter. I scanned it and put the original in a file."

He folded the changing mat. "Did you clean this?"

Elle nodded.

"Thanks. Remind me to send you flowers for putting up with me today."

She chuckled. "It will cost you more than flowers, which I would end up ordering myself anyway."

"Probably right, which reminds me … Where do I get more diapers and stuff?"

"The same place you order groceries. I assume you order groceries. Alan does." She laid the baby in the car seat and buckled the harness. Adam adjusted the buckle and shifted the baby in the seat, then tucked a blanket around her.

"Where did you learn how to do that?" asked Elle.

"The baby-safety class we took before the Crawfords had Joy. Properly putting a child in a car seat requires attention to detail. There wasn't a base with this carrier, was there?"

"No. Should there be?"

"I can secure the seat in my SUV without it, but using the base would be better."

"I left the bottle in the fridge. I'll meet you out front." Elle hurried from the room.

Adam put on a spare jacket before slinging the diaper bag over his shoulder and grabbing the carrier by the handle. Andrew and Alan waited near the reception desk, not hiding their smiles. Elle handed him the bottle as the phone rang. Adam simply nodded at his brothers, not wanting to start a conversation.

"Adam! You need to take this." Elle held up the phone.

Adam took the phone with his free hand. "Mr. Adam speaking."

"Adam Hastings? This is Dr. Tamara Brooks from the behavioral-health unit at Eastland hospital. Do you have a moment?"

Raindrops raced down the window. September traced a trail with her finger. Would he come? Dr. Brooks had said he would be here by three o'clock. The clock above the nurse's station read 2:55. Her labs had come back clear, and the lactation specialist had given her permission to nurse Harmony after reviewing the medication Dr. Brooks prescribed. She had skipped pumping an hour ago and was ready to feed her baby. An SUV pulled into the parking lot. She pressed closer to the window to see a man in a heavy coat climb out and open the back door. He emerged with a car seat covered with a blanket she didn't recognize. The man turned and looked up at the hospital.

Adam.

She turned from the window and took a deep breath.

The practiced words left her mind as she waited in the silent room. Dr. Brooks had pointed out there were other things besides the postpartum depression September needed to work through. One of them was dealing with the father of her baby. September hadn't mentioned to the doctor that the man who now carried her daughter into the hospital wasn't the father. But she needed to talk to him worse than she did Harmony's biological father. Only three other people in the world knew the identity of the birth father—the man who didn't want Harmony; September's manager, who wished the child and its father didn't exist; and the woman who'd helped her hide from both these past months.

September paced the room. How long would it take Adam and Harmony to get through security? Adam couldn't bring his keys, phone, or gun into the unit. Purses and bags were not allowed beyond security either. She wasn't sure what that meant for Harmony's diaper bag.

She smoothed the front of the pink nursing top. The boxy top was more flattering than the gray scrubs but barely, as it was made of the same material and general shape. Not that flattering would help. The mirror confirmed the fact earlier, showing her a face worthy of a bait click blog, "Where is September, and What Does She Look Like Now?" She barely resembled her last round of publicity photos. A good thing because sooner or later, even with HIPAA laws, someone was bound to recognize her and divulge the news.

The door opened, and September turned to face her future and her past.

Mother nature kicked in at the sight of Harmony, and September crossed her arms to hold the flannel nursing pads in place. "Thanks for coming and bringing Harmony." She held out her arms, wishing she could hold them both. But she'd given up the opportunity to hold the man long ago.

Adam shifted the baby in his arms. The carrier must not have been able to leave the security area. "She is sleeping."

September sank into the glider rocker. Her arms still empty, she pointed to the sofa next to her. "Sit for a moment?"

Adam took up more than half the sofa. She had forgotten how big he was, but his size had never intimidated her. Even now, knowing she needed to explain things, she wasn't scared. How different he was from—she couldn't follow that line of thinking.

"I owe you an explanation. Thank you for taking Harmony." She swallowed back the emotion. "I have postpartum depression, and the only safe place I knew for her to be was with you." There. She'd said the words Dr. Brooks had encouraged her to. She took a deep breath before adding what he needed to understand. "I tried to kill us."

"I'm glad you chose a different option."

Adam struggled to keep his face passive. He suspected September's situation had escalated to dire from Dr. Brooks' call a few hours ago, but thoughts of suicide and infanticide were beyond what he'd expected. Internet searches had helped him fill in the gaps. A phone call to his mother had backed up the articles. For many women, a new baby wasn't as joyful as a Hearthfire movie made motherhood seem. He'd been surprised to learn his mother had also been under a therapist's care after Alex and Abbie were born. From the moment he walked into the room, he knew that whatever September was experiencing, it wasn't an act. Her eyes were dull, devoid of their usual sparkle, the brown more reminiscent of mud than the gingerbread he remembered. Her hair hung limply around her face and was longer than a year ago, the ends split and frizzy. At first he thought she had two black eyes, but once she sat down, he recognized the dark circles as signs of extreme fatigue. Dozens of questions raced through his mind. Unfortunately, Dr. Brooks had cautioned him not to ask any. "The most important part of this visit is to reassure the mother the baby still accepts her."

She rubbed her arms. "Shyla will kill me if she ever finds out, especially if my being here leaks to the tabloids. I am registered under my real name, but they are using my middle name, Rayne. I need you to use it too."

Interesting that the manager didn't know where she was. How had September managed that? Shyla always hovered around September with the persistence of a starving mosquito. "I think I can remember to call you Rayne." The baby stirred and stretched in his arms.

September held out her arms. "Please?"

Adam stood and settled the child in September's arms.

"Hey, sweetheart, Mommy missed you. But I put you in a safe place just like I said I would."

Adam strained to hear what she was saying.

"Do you like Adam? Some people think he is big and scary."

The baby turned to face her mother. September raised her head. "Please hand me the blanket."

She draped the blanket over her shoulder and covered the baby's head. His first reaction was to snatch the blanket back to keep her from suffocating the child, but then he realized she intended to nurse the baby. Adam studied the print on the wall as little sucking noises filled the room.

"Don't look so worried. I am covered. They gave me a special nursing shirt, so I am not about to flash you. I made some poor choices after you left, but I am still not that kind of girl."

"Thank you, I—" The questions burned his throat, but he held them in.

"I understand Harmony's existence will shatter my reputation. When Shyla learned about my pregnancy, she went ballistic and tried to force me to…which I refused. I don't know what her plan is for me to return to the stage. I'm afraid if she finds out I am here, she will try to get Harmony taken from me. The only reason she is helping me at all is because of my money. She isn't the person I thought she was. But you warned me about her, didn't you?"

Adam only nodded. He hadn't been on the job long before he'd understood the biggest threat to September's life wasn't some crazed fan trying to touch her but the manipulation she had lived with for years from her "loving" manager. He had tried to explain the danger to the music star, but September couldn't see the truth.

"She thinks I am in Seattle. After what she asked me to do, I can't work with her, but because of our agreement, I believe I need to wait for the contract to expire before I can get rid of her. She knows too much for me to fire her, so I am stuck with her for two more years. Right now I am paying her to keep her mouth shut."

Adam clamped his jaw to keep from asking what the doctor asked him not to.

She draped the baby over her leg and patted her back. "Come on, give Mama a big burp and you can eat more."

A belch loud enough to make a ten-year-old jealous echoed throughout the room.

"I thought you were supposed to burp babies over your shoulder." Adam hoped burping was a safe topic.

"According to my midwife, there isn't a proper way. She picks up a baby with her palm on the baby's chest and gets the most amazing burps. I've tried it, but I think my hand is too small. Your hands might work." September positioned the baby on her other side, and Adam studied the back of the door.

"We are covered. I told you I wasn't going to flash you. Did Harmony do all right with the bottle?"

"I'm not sure. She spit up a lot and kept pushing the bottle out of her mouth. Mom will be back tomorrow, and she can teach me more. I think she kept some in because she slept."

"I'm kinda glad she didn't take to it. I'm worried she will switch over and not need me. I didn't realize the hospital would allow her up here with me before I checked in. My doctor didn't mention the pilot program. Patients' babies can stay on the floor from 7:00 a.m. to 7:00 p.m. They have someone to take care of them in a special nursery. Dr. Brooks' philosophy is that having the baby nearby and having the new moms take care of them as much as we are able helps us to heal faster. If we get overwhelmed, help is right there." She looked down at her daughter. The baby reached a tiny hand toward her mother's face. Though invited, he felt like he was intruding on something special. September looked up and caught him staring. "I do love her very much. But there is something not quite right with me. Every time she cries, I want to cry. Then she cries and cries and I think crazy things. But then I experience a moment like this, and I can see how crazy I was. Please don't think less of me for doing what I did."

"Choosing to check yourself in shows you are brave and strong." He repeated the words Dr. Brooks had used. "I don't understand why you chose me to care for your daughter, but I will support you." Emotions he'd never felt before threatened to cut off his air supply as September lowered her head and talked to her daughter again. For months he'd told himself he had done the right thing by walking away. There was no way they could have made a relationship work—was there?

The minute hand moved again, their time almost over. Harmony's breathing changed, the little sucking noises now quiet. Letting her daughter go this time would be almost as hard as it was early this morning. But this morning she'd thought she would be without her daughter for days. Now she had hope she could learn the skills she needed and keep her daughter with her much of the time. September needed to clear her first twenty-four hours before she and Harmony would be assigned to the PPD unit. There would be more counseling sessions if Adam agreed to continue to play father, but that could get very awkward.

"You are probably wondering about the note."

"It has crossed my mind a few times." His folded arms were not a good sign.

"I try not to lie."

"I believe you called it 'fudging the truth.'"

"I'm not ready to explain, but please believe I chose you for Harmony's sake."

He closed his eyes and leaned back. He was thinking. How quickly his mannerisms came back to her. "I'm not supposed to ask you questions, but I need to know—are you or the baby in danger?"

How should she answer? "I received a very credible death threat."

Adam raised his brows. "Can you tell me more?"

Not here, not now. She shook her head slightly. The light by the door indicated someone was monitoring their conversation. If he was the same Adam, her not answering would make him wonder, and if he wondered, he would go find the answer himself. For now, that would have to do. She moved Harmony to her lap and straightened her top before removing the blanket. "This is how the midwife burped her." September attempted the one-handed lift while supporting her daughter's head and back with the other hand. "See? I can't get this method to work."

Adam reached over and took Harmony from her. "Let me try." He lifted Harmony using the hold she had demonstrated, and the expected belch came. He smiled as big as if he'd produced the sound himself. "I hope it works with the bottle too."

"If you get all the air out, she is less likely to spit up." She handed the blanket to him. "I'm not sure when they will ask you to come back. Dr. Brooks says I need to complete my twenty-four-hour evaluation period first. Normally they don't allow visitors the first day, but they want to see if allowing PPD mothers a few minutes with our babies the first day will help with overall recovery time."

"That is what they told me on the phone. Don't worry about your little one. I'll keep her safe."

"I know you will. Despite everything, that is the one thing I know." She stood and crossed to the door where she pressed the buzzer. "I'll see you both tomorrow."

Fortunately, the attendant arrived before any tears started to fall. At least she hadn't cried in the room with Adam and Harmony. She didn't need him seeing how crazy she was—no, not crazy. Depressed. Dr. Brooks specifically said she wasn't crazy. But it sure felt that way.

ADAM RETRIEVED HIS PHONE AND keys while a caregiver changed the baby's diaper. Dr. Brooks waited for him near security. "That went well. Rayne had bonded with her baby prior to coming to our facility. Sometimes with PPD moms, bonding doesn't happen in the first few weeks. After talking to Rayne, though, I thought she might have. Not all PPD mothers want to keep their children with them or have managed to bond. A positive bonding can improve the response to PPD treatment and recovery. I will contact you tomorrow afternoon and ask you to bring Harmony up for several hours. You will not need to stay; in fact, we prefer if you don't stay beyond the transfer conversation."

"Transfer conversation?"

"I encourage the mothers to ask about their children and what happened in their time apart, even if the report is only hours slept and bottles consumed. I find it is helpful if the other parent can give a few more details—not that I expect babies at this age to laugh or speak or anything. When you pick Harmony up, we encourage the same conversation. Only this time with you asking the questions."

"I thought you didn't want me asking questions."

"I don't want you asking questions with no answers. Even doctors don't understand why some women get PPD and others don't. Asking Rayne questions about herself she isn't prepared to answer will not be helpful. I understand the two of you are not married, but I would like you to give serious thought to what happens after Rayne's release. We normally ask the mothers and their partners to take a parenting class and attend family counseling sessions. Having a father figure is very important to the development of your daughter. I hope you take this into consideration."

Adam nodded. There wasn't a good answer for what she was asking or assuming. The nurse returned with the baby already fastened in the car carrier. "Thank you for changing her. I still am working on that skill. And, Doctor, thank you for your thoughts." He double-checked the car seat harness before leaving.

"Mr. Adam—I mean Hastings ..."

"Mr. Adam is fine."

"I have one more concern about you and Harmony. Not once today in our phone conversation or here at the unit have I heard you say your daughter's name. If you are going to bond with her, you need to start calling her Harmony. Not 'her' or 'the baby.' Even nicknames are powerful."

He nodded again and exited the building before he received any more advice. Taking care of September's baby was one thing. Playing the father ... well, he wasn't quite ready for that.

He drove away from the hospital, pesky what-if questions filling his mind. He turned down one street, then another, not eager to arrive at any particular destination. At some point he realized the baby had fallen asleep, so he kept driving one suburb after another. He'd never noticed Chicago had so many toy stores and establishments dedicated to infants and children. He should get a base for the car seat, but he didn't want to wake the baby up to go into the store. Maybe he would run out and get one later. The doctor was right. He wasn't thinking of September's baby as Harmony. Why should he? Bonding with the child wasn't on his to-do list. The officer had been wrong in her assessment that he would be a good father because he'd worried about the baby first. The baby was a client. Getting too close to a client was never a good idea. If he had stayed aloof with September, he never would have kissed her. He would still be working for her, and she would be out on tour someplace instead of in a hospital and hiding a newborn from the world. Her pregnancy was not his doing. Maybe he could have handled things better. His growing attraction had turned into a distraction, and he'd nearly missed the stalker fan wielding the small knife. If his partner hadn't shouted the warning, he would not have gotten to September in time and the small scar on his arm could have been a much larger scar on September's face—or worse. He'd left her for her own safety. The kiss had proven the depth of his feelings, and the only way he could control those feelings was to not be around her.

Eventually, he reached his parents' neighborhood. A black SUV he didn't recognize sat in their driveway. He parked next to it, and his sister opened the front door of the house. He pointed to the black SUV. "New vehicle?"

"No, new driver. Hurry up. I have things to show you." Abbie closed the storm door and waited inside, protected from the cold February air.

Adam grabbed the baby in the car seat and the diaper bag and hurried into the house. He set them both on the floor before pulling his sister into a hug. "What are you doing here, and where is your driver?"

"He is in the kitchen, and before you ask, he carried the boxes in, not me. And you can report to Mom that I am not carrying any weapons today." She gestured to the four large moving boxes at the center of the living room.

"What? No gun? Did your husband promise to buy you an island?" Adam removed the blanket draped over the infant carrier, relieved to find the baby still sleeping.

"No, Preston isn't buying me an island. Although he did bribe me with a week in Hawaii at the end of the month if the doctor lets me go. It was you who convinced me to stop carrying, at least for a while."

"Me?" Adam held up his hand. "I've been staying out of this little argument." *Little* wasn't the right word. Preston Harmon's head of security, Simon Dermot, had appealed to Jethro Hastings for help. The first couple of months of her marriage, his sister had not made things easy for her bodyguards. Understandable since she'd spent years guarding rather than being guarded, but as the wife of the heir to the Harmon Media universe, she'd become a target of desperate and jealous people. Her husband's concern had grown as her pregnancy progressed. When Preston learned he had fathered triplets, he'd begged Abbie to stop trying to be her own bodyguard.

"Mom and I had a heart-to-heart before Grandma fell and broke her hip. She told me a very interesting story. When you were about nine months old, Mom was still wearing a concealed knife. One afternoon she fell asleep while feeding you. Somehow you found the knife and worked it free of its sheath. Mom woke up to you screaming. The blade had nicked your leg, and you were bleeding. She didn't carry any weapons again until Andrew started school. Although I still have twenty weeks before this trio makes their appearance, I've been trying to get used to not having my gun on me." Abbie placed her hand on her rounding belly.

"I have the scar. I asked Mom about it when I was about five, and she got all weepy. Dad told me the story and asked me not to talk about my scar ever again. I've probably helped you avoid a potential disaster."

"Probably. From what I have been reading about triplets, it is almost impossible to childproof things. One woman's triplets helped each other escape their cribs and room when they were about eighteen months old. They made it to the kitchen where they proceeded to make a mess. One of them picked up the landline and accidentally dialed 911. The police showed up at three in the morning. The poor mother was worried the incident would be reported to child services."

The baby stirred, and Abbie leaned down and pulled her out of her car seat. "What I am worried about is all those times Mom said, 'I hope you get one just like you.' Since the rest of you don't seem inclined to matrimony, I am afraid the triplets might be a way of paying you guys back using nephews." She stood back up, cradling the baby in her arms, her voice rising half an octave as she spoke toward the baby. "But now you have this little angel, which isn't fair because I was the angel of the family."

Adam laughed. "More like the mini manipulator. You had us all doing your bidding. Most of the inventive ideas we executed originated with you—like tying the wagon between two bikes. And Mom still believes I was behind the build-a-raft-and-cross-to-Canada-it-will-be-fun day."

"How old was I? Four? I had no clue Canada was far away. At least you could read." Abbie held her middle and laughed.

Startled by their laughter, the baby scrunched her face and let out a wail.

"Oh, did the big man scare you with his lies?" Abbie rocked the baby, then scrunched her own nose. "I think it is time for the big man to change your diaper. He needs more practice."

"Again? She got changed before we got in the car." Adam dug through the diaper bag for another diaper. Only two left. "After I change her, do you mind watching her while I run to the store? I seem to need more diapers."

"I would love to hang out with Harmony. We can look inside the boxes of stuff Auntie Mandy sent." Abbie handed the baby over to Adam.

"Mandy sent all of this?" The wife of one of Hasting Security's longest-term clients had once been Abbie's to protect. They had become friends long before Abbie married.

"Mandy boxed everything up to donate to charity. It is stuff Joy has grown out of or duplicate gifts she received. She's been waiting until I found out the gender of these three before donating. And since I don't need any girl clothes, you are welcome to take your pick. There were a few things I would have kept, but Preston's mum might not survive the word *hand-me-down* for her grandbabies. I think she is buying up half of Europe as we speak."

Adam shook his head. "Do you and Mandy realize hand-me-downs are not something normal in the way upper 1 percent?"

Abbie laughed. "Chicago society might never be the same because of the two of us, and now with Candace married to Colin, no telling what will happen to Chicago's upper crust."

"As long as you don't create a scandal, they will survive. But a few might skip your parties." Adam shook his head as he walked upstairs to the room his mother had set up as a grandbaby paradise. This diaper changing went much better, with no clothing damaged in the process. Maybe he could figure out this baby thing after all.

The breast pump beeped. September checked the bag.

Empty.

Empty arms.

Empty heart.

She tried to pump before going to sleep. The bottles were almost empty.

If only her dreams were empty too.

The aisle of diapers went on forever. Adam pulled out his phone and texted Abbie.

What kind of diapers should I buy?

— Mandy likes the ones in the red box.
What size?
— Get 2 size ones and one size 2.
That many?
— 3 isn't that many. Oh, don't forget a couple boxes of wipes.
— and formula
— and diaper rash cream. There is none in the bag.
Anything else?
— Not tonight.

Adam pulled the policewoman's card out of his pocket and found the formula she'd recommended. Did he need another bottle, too? The last time he was in the Crawford's kitchen, there had been several draining on the sideboard. There had only been one in the diaper bag. The bottle display was more confusing than the diaper section. Its color coding and nipple shapes made little sense. He picked up one brand after another.

A woman with two children in her cart stopped next to him. "New baby?"

"Ya, kind of."

"Six to eight weeks, I'd guess by the diapers. Trying to choose the first bottle?"

"Yes, her mom had been—" He felt the heat rise in his neck. Was it appropriate to discuss nursing with a stranger?

The woman picked up a bottle and a set of nipples. "Try these. All of my kids liked them the best. If this is the first bottle, you might want three or four."

"Thanks."

The woman chose a pacifier for her own cart.

"Should I get one of those, too?" asked Adam.

"Don't start one if you don't need to. Getting them to quit is a pain." The woman rolled her eyes, then moved her cart down the aisle.

Adam paused at a display of toys at the end of the section. A little pink giraffe stared up at him. He picked the animal up.

The plush fur felt as soft as it looked. The tag indicated the toy was approved for children under three. He set it back down. He only needed basics.

The giraffe stared up at him again.

He added it to the cart.

No cry woke September in the middle of the night, but the absence of a cry did. September wandered out of her room to the nurses' station. "Is there a pump I can use?"

A nurse led her into the room September had used earlier in the day. One of the other mothers sat there, along with a lactation consultant. "Pump enough to be comfortable. Chances are by the time you go home, your baby won't need middle-of-the-night feedings, so it is fine if your body decides it doesn't need to give them."

September longed to trade the silicone and plastic for the warm sleepy tones of her daughter. Was Harmony awake and crying? Had Adam figured out how to feed her, or had Adam's mother come back to town? September took a deep breath. Adam was the best choice, he would figure it out. A bottle had to be easier than nursing. She repeated the thought over and over, not wanting to panic in front of the others.

She turned off the pump, and the consultant helped her label the milk for storage to go home with Harmony after the next visit. September found her way back to her room under the watchful eye of the nurse at the station.

As she fell back asleep, she reassured herself, *Adam is the best choice. He will figure it out.*

THE FORMULA SCOOP BOUNCED ON the tile floor, white powder spilling everywhere as Harmony's cries amplified. Adam balanced her on his shoulder as he reached for the scoop, which he kicked rather than picked up. The sound of footsteps in the hallway caused him to turn. "Sorry, Da—"

His father put his finger to his lips, walked to the sink, turned on the over-sink light, then turned off the main kitchen light. Without saying a word, he took Harmony from Adam and hummed to her as he paced the floor, quieting her.

Adam washed and dried the scoop before measuring out the formula and making a fresh bottle. Jethro took the bottle from Adam and tested it by squirting some milk on the back of his hand. He mouthed the word "sweep" before going into the living room. Adam stared at the empty doorway for several seconds before retrieving the broom from the pantry. The powder didn't sweep up well, and he tried a wet paper towel before thinking it through. The wet powder dissolved, creating an even bigger mess in the dim light. Not knowing where his father had gone, he didn't dare turn on the light to find the mop and ended up scrubbing on his hands and knees. When he finished, he went in search of his father and Harmony.

When he found them, he wished he had his phone so he could take a photo. Harmony's head was tucked into his father's neck. His dad's mouth hung open, snoring filling the room. On the table next to his father's chair sat the empty bottle. Worried his father might startle and drop the baby, Adam extracted Harmony from Jethro's arms and took her up to her crib. When he came back down, his father was at the sink, rinsing out the bottle.

"Where did you learn to do that, Dad?"

"Five children. You don't think I let your mom have all the fun, did you? Wrangling Abbie and Alex required more than two hands. Especially with you and Alan running around like Wile E. and the Road Runner." He put the bottle on the drying rack. "Next time, don't turn on every light in the house. They tend to agitate a little one, and it is harder to feed a crying baby than a calm one."

"Thanks, Dad."

"Night, son."

Adam checked on Harmony. The little giraffe sat on the dresser near the crib. Abbie had been a wealth of information about everything from the baby sleeping on her back to not putting a blanket in the crib. She'd even left an already worn copy of a baby-care book for him to reference. By the time her children came, Adam assumed she would have read the entire parenting section of the bookstore.

He looked at his clock as he climbed back into bed: 3:24. Poor September. Had she done this all alone every night? He pulled out his phone and read the report his brother had sent.

No evidence of bodyguards in California for past seven months. Consistent with Shyla's story of rehab.

Rumor in area of her hiring private security. Dermot says not their job. But lost their only female guard to someone about six months ago.

A house purchased in September's mother's maiden name; trust in Chicago-suburb gated community. Assuming it is hers.

Each piece of the puzzle made the bigger picture. If only he had known.

It all came back to the kiss. What if he had tried to work it out? The ten-year gap in their ages had shrunk as she'd grown older. Twenty to thirty had been a world apart, but twenty-six to thirty-six seemed more manageable. The existence of Harmony shrunk the perceived age difference even more. If only he'd seen things this way a year ago when he'd kissed her and unleashed all the feelings he had bottled up for so long. He'd tried to apologize the next morning, but the words had come out all wrong. Then she said things she probably didn't mean, and he'd quit. If he could erase just ten minutes of his life, it wouldn't be the truth in the kiss. It would be the lies afterward.

He pulled up the blanket, rolled over on his side, and closed his eyes—just seconds before a cry came from the room down the hall.

Group therapy, though the words conjured scenes of television AA meetings, turned out to be nothing September anticipated. Still, it was hard to be open and honest when she wasn't even using the name the world knew her by. Two women discussed how their spouses didn't understand or have any desire to help them. As near as September could tell, she was the only one in the room who had been attempting to single parent without the support of her parents or the child's father. Her live-in housekeeper and visits from Melanie Hastings were good but not the same.

Dr. Brooks shared enough about her own recovery to give them hope. Postpartum depression, unlike other types of depression, had a known beginning and end. Right before the session concluded, Leisha asked a question. "When I got married three years ago, we discussed having three children. But I am afraid if I have more, it will get worse."

"While there is no telling exactly how your body will react with future children, most women are able to successfully raise families after a PPD diagnosis. One of the keys is early recognition and treatment. There are many elements to recovery, including stress factors beyond motherhood. Sorry there are no blanket answers for next time. Each case will need to be handled individually." Dr. Brooks looked each mom in the eye before concluding the session. "Now, for most of you, it is time for some baby-and-me time, followed by lunch. Those of you who are nursing, remember that as much as we try to make it homey here, your babies notice the underlying hospital smell and know something is different. They also are getting more supplemental bottles. Just love them and don't worry if they aren't eating. If you get frustrated, remember, help is nearby."

September followed the others out of the room. One of the aides stood near the door. "Rayne? Your daughter is here. If you will come with me."

Adam stood in the middle of the room they were in yesterday with Harmony in his arms, his focus on the baby. "There she is, just like I told you." He spoke in soft tones before placing her into September's waiting arms.

"How was she last night?"

"Once the bumbling idiot, yours truly, figured out how to make a bottle, she did fine. Dad fed her, and they both fell asleep. I wish I'd had my phone to take a photo."

"Your dad? I can't picture it." September smoothed the top of Harmony's head. She smelled fresh, like the baby wash she'd put in the diaper bag.

"Well, he had plenty of practice with the five of us, and with Abbie expecting triplets, he probably needs more."

"I thought the triplet thing was a tabloid joke." In her experience, tabloids only published enough carefully worded truth not to get sued.

Adam put one hand in his jeans pocket. "No, only the part about being fathered by an alien."

He smiled one of those half smiles she missed so much. The cheeky smile in a photo on his mother's phone had invited her to entertain a crush before they'd even met.

"I probably should go."

"You'll be back around six thirty or seven?"

"Dr. Brooks told me six thirty. Security had me leave the diaper bag at the check-in station. I brought two extra outfits in case little Miss Harmony decides she needs to wear separate outfits after each meal." When his voice softened as he said her daughter's name, a lump came to her throat, and warmth filled her chest.

He stopped at the doorway. "Oh, Abbie brought over some clothing her friend's baby grew out of, so if you don't recognize some of the outfits in the bag, that is why."

September swallowed before speaking. "Tell Abbie thanks. I have more clothes for Harmony at home, but I grabbed just what was on the dresser and stuffed it in the bag since I needed to leave fast." Before my demons caught up with me.

"Don't worry about it. Abbie is having all boys but keeps finding things for girls. I wouldn't be surprised if she doesn't still find a thing or two she can't resist buying."

"Your sister is so fun. Tell her not to buy too much." She didn't worry about Abbie spending too much money—not possible for a billionaire's wife—but she didn't want to feel any more awkward around the Hastings family when she got out.

"I will. Anything else you need?"

"I can wear my own clothes as long as they don't have drawstrings. When your mom gets back, will you please ask her to go get some from the house?" She froze, wondering how much he already knew.

"Mom knows where you live?"

He didn't know. Melanie had promised not to let even Jethro know, but part of September doubted she would keep everything secret. "Um, yes. Your mom helped me buy it."

"Well, she is due in this afternoon. I'll let her know. Anything particular you want?"

"Nursing tops. But T-shirts and button-downs work. And two pairs of jeans, a pair of sweats, and some underwear, please."

His Adam's apple bobbed before he answered. "I think I'll let Mom pick those out for you."

"The base to Harmony's car seat is in my car in the garage. I took an Uber to your office and here." Actually, she had taken three, all under an assumed name. She'd met the first one outside a house three doors down so he wouldn't see where she lived. "I'd better go. She is hungry." September hurried from the room before he could ask any more questions she didn't want to answer. Like how much his mother knew.

Harmony made the pinched-face look she got right before she cried. September entered the nursing area filled with chairs and rockers. Madison already sat with other moms. Leisha's twins had a cold and wouldn't be coming up today, so she was nowhere to be seen. September joined the women as they chatted and nursed and pumped. Something in the camaraderie made the task easier than two days ago in the solitude of her house. Or perhaps the meds had kicked in, or seeing Adam's smile had boosted her mood. September didn't care about the why, as long as her personal storm clouds continued to float away.

ADAM PICKED UP HIS KEYS and phone from the security desk. There were three texts, the first from his mother.

—Please pick me up at O'Hare at 3:30. Usual spot.

The next was from his father.

—Your mother lands at 3:10 pick her up at 3:30. Usual spot.

The last was from Elle at the office.

— I have three phone messages for you. Please call when you can.

He answered yes to the first two texts, then called Elle once he reached the privacy of the car. "Hey, it's Adam. What's up?"

"Mrs. Hastings called. She needs you to pick her up at 3:30." Three requests. Unusual for Mom. "Alex called. He wondered if you could take a shift tomorrow afternoon. He needs someone to fill in during a dental appointment."

"Do you know who the client is?"

"Daniel Crawford and Colin Ogilvie have off-site meetings to attend with Galli-Batiste International."

Adam double-checked his calendar. Harmony should be with September all afternoon. "I think I can as long as I am done by five."

"Fine, I'll put you on the schedule. The last one isn't really a call. Jethro asked you to call Simon Dermot at Dermot Security. He said Mr. Dermot has some information for you. Also, Alan wants to know if you are coming in today." Adam checked his watch. If he went to the office, he would only be there an hour or so before heading to the airport. "Does he need something specific?"

"One moment. I'll check." Elle's voice faded out. She must have pressed the mute button, meaning Alan stood next to her. "Alan is trying out a new surveillance system and wants testers."

"Tell Alan I can in the morning. I don't dare risk missing mom's flight because some electronic gadget locked me in a room." He heard a snatch of conversation through his phone.

"Alan says that will work."

"Tell Alan to get back to work." Wouldn't help, even though Alan maintained his interest in his client-turned-secretary was platonic. A lie only Alan believed. "Thanks, Elle."

Adam dialed Simon Dermot's number. Until last year, he had always felt Hastings was competing with Simon's security firm. However, after Abbie's stint as an undercover fake fiancée for Simon's biggest client, Preston Harmon, his respect for them had grown. Watching his sister via phone conference as she and Simon disabled a bomb had a lot to do with the trust he had in the other firm. Now she was married to Preston, and Dermot was in charge of Abbie's security. There wasn't another firm on earth he would trust with Abbie's life. "Hey, Simon, it's Adam Hastings."

"Thanks for calling back. Your father asked me to poke around, and I have a few answers. After Hastings Security parted ways with September Pratt, an LA firm, Armstrong Security, was hired. They are fairly large, the type of place where the boss doesn't know everyone. The day before September's manager, Shyla, announced she was going into rehab, the firm was put on standby, meaning they were not actively serving as her protection. Then, four months ago, ties were severed with Armstrong, and a new startup by the generic name of Smith's Best Bodyguards was hired. They are on retainer, although September has still not made any appearances and reportedly isn't in LA. According to California business records, Smith's Best founder is Sven Bent, who worked for Armstrong until the day they were put on standby."

"Sounds suspicious."

"That's what I thought. I could keep digging, but I think I hit a nerve and my contact at Armstrong clammed up. A general search on Sven didn't come up with anything, but I can't find him before three years ago. Sorry I don't have more for you."

"Thanks, Simon. That is a start."

"No problem. Later."

The line went dead. Adam left the Eastland hospital parking lot and headed toward the office. He called Alan's private cell on the hands-free. "Are you alone?"

"Not at the moment. But give me a minute." *Still at the reception desk*?

Adam waited for his brother to speak again.

"There. I am in my office, and, no, I wasn't flirting with ZoElle."

"You realize you are the only one who calls her by her full name? Don't answer. Not why I called. There is a new security firm in LA called Smith's Best. I need everything you can find on them and the owner—a Sven Bent."

"Again?"

"What do you mean 'again'?"

"Mom asked for the same thing four or five months ago for one of her clients."

"Mom is consulting? She hasn't been in the office at all."

"She must be doing it on the side. Had me bill her for my time."

"And this didn't raise any red flags?" Adam pulled into a nearby parking lot.

"No, Mom takes jobs a few times a year. Clients needing more privacy than security. The type of thing people don't want to go through our office for but all on the up-and-up. I know better than to ask questions."

"I didn't realize she had clients of her own other than the ones she consults with us for." When he thought about it, her side job made sense. Mom was an expert at setting up complicated security plans, and he knew she had contracted for Simon in the past. "So, what do you have on him?"

"No can do. Ask Mom. She said if anyone—especially you—asked, only she could answer. She even password-protected the file."

Adam wished he had gone into the office. It was always easier to intimidate his brother in person. He checked the dash. One hour and fifty minutes until he could pick his mother up. "Thanks for not so much."

"Anytime, bro."

Adam headed to the nearest gun range. Target practice was a good way to work out his frustrations about the puzzle that was growing more complicated with every question.

September curled up with her feet beneath her in the big chair. Harmony had been sleeping when she left her in the nursery. Initially, she worried the care would not be adequate, but the nurses and caregivers cooed and fussed over each baby as they cared for them. They showed September what they were doing and even a trick for changing Harmony's diaper faster.

Dr. Brooks sat across from her in another chair, feet crossed at the ankles. "Rayne, we often find that PPD mothers also carry stress from past experiences. I am aware your parents died when you were fifteen and you are not married to the father of your child. Both can cause stress in a new mom. Is there anything else I should know about you that may exasperate your postpartum depression?"

"My career is demanding. Everyone is always looking to see if I'll slip up. I miss a note and Twitter gets a new hashtag. I wear a color that clashes with my eyes and the blogosphere turns my shirt color into the event of the week. I miss a dance move and it becomes a meme. I have been hiding out these past months under the guise of needing to detox. I have never done drugs, but with my reputation as a Christian singer with a virtuous lifestyle, my manager felt the truth would be worse for my career than the lie." September paused. Shyla had wanted her to terminate the pregnancy at a private clinic near Puget Sound, but with Melanie Hastings' help, September had ditched her guard in the Seattle Tacoma airport and rerouted to Chicago via rental car and train. The email to Shyla composed with Melanie's help left her manager with little choice other than to accept and perpetuate the lie. "When I do return to work, I don't want to hide Harmony, but I don't know if I am strong enough to face the world. They will be merciless. My manager, Shyla, spent so much time exploiting my commitment to be a virtuous woman as part of my marketing. I think fans will feel I let them down. The thing I am most afraid of is all those teen girls who idealize me and wear purity rings because of my songs."

"That is a lot to carry. Do you have any other family support? Adam?"

"Adam's mother, Melanie, took me under her wing when my parents died. She has been there for me most of the past ten years. Adam was stationed in the Middle East when they died, and he was in the army for a few more years after that. I didn't get to know him until about five years ago." She didn't want the doctor to think with the ten-year gap between their ages that anything had been going on when she was still a minor. Even last year the age gap had become one of the main reasons Adam left her. He didn't see how the difference between twenty-five and thirty-five wasn't nearly like fifteen and twenty-five.

Dr. Brooks raised her brows for the smallest of seconds. "That would be why you used her as your contact person?"

"Yes, she has helped me with everything the past six months. If her mother hadn't fallen and broken her hip, she would have been here when I checked in. I asked them to call her and give her my code so she could contact me. She called last night and told me her mother was doing well and her sister was there, so she was coming back. I'm glad she'll be here to help with Harmony."

"Don't you have confidence her father can take care of her?"

September studied her hands. If Harmony's father even knew about her existence ..."Adam is still learning." It was as diplomatic of an answer as she could give.

"Rayne." Dr. Brooks looked at her notes before continuing. "Adam isn't the father, is he?"

September froze. "Why would you think that?"

"Whenever I ask you a question about Harmony's father, you deflect or word your answer carefully. I noticed in the couple conversations I've had with him, he is also very careful."

The doctor didn't have any hard evidence. Would Family Services get involved if they thought Adam wasn't the father? She had only dealt with them briefly after her parents' death and didn't want them involved in Harmony's life. Shyla and the Hastings had helped her file for emancipated minor status, keeping her out of the system. But she had heard the horror stories in the news. "Since we aren't married, the situation is awkward."

"Another evasive answer. Who is listed as the father on Harmony's birth certificate?"

"No one. Since I am not married, I didn't have to name a father and felt that would be best."

Dr. Brooks made a note.

Panic. Melanie had double-checked the law before proposing the plan, but what if they'd missed something?

"Although Harmony's birth seems to have some anomalies, there is nothing I need to report to the state or Family Services. Even if Adam isn't the genetic father, you chose him to care for your baby, and he seems to be doing well in that role. Nowhere in your forms did you write that he is the father, so there is no legal misrepresentation. My biggest concern is the family-therapy portion of your care. Should your sessions include Adam and his mother, or will they not be in your life once you are discharged?"

Outside of the window, the rain fell, obliterating the last of the snow until the next storm. "I am sure Melanie will be there. I am not so sure about Adam, but he is the kind of man with integrity, so whatever he says he will do, he will do." Even if it means walking away from his heart. She admired his personal code of honor and loved him for it, even if it kept them apart.

"Very interesting word choice. I don't think I've heard the word *integrity* to define a significant other in quite some time. If he participates in family therapy with you, I'll keep that in mind. Enough of my grilling. What concerns you most?"

September asked the question plaguing her for weeks. "What if I can never be a good mom?"

THE DASHBOARD CLOCK READ 3:27 as Adam pulled up to the curb. Melanie Hastings waited next to her large, pink, wheeled suitcase. She said she liked to use pink because no one else in the family would touch it. It had kept him from grabbing the more convenient item over the years. Adam opened the back door of his SUV and tossed the bag in. If necessary, he could keep it as ransom. He gave his mother a hug and received a kiss on the cheek before getting back into the driver's seat.

"How is Grandma?"

"Busy as ever. Do you want to skip the small talk?"

"Yup. September said you helped her buy her house. And when I asked Alan to run a background check on something odd related to September, he wouldn't tell me anything. Said I had to talk to you. So I am talking."

"There wasn't a question in there."

"Mom." He knew he sounded like a frustrated five-year-old, but some habits died hard. "You are only going to tell me what you planned to. Do I have to find the right questions, too?"

"Maybe I should ask the questions. What do you know?"

"I'm assuming September was never in rehab and she has been in the Chicago area for some time. For whatever reason, probably involving Harmony, she has cut ties with Shyla. I think she hired you about the time she disappeared, but even Dad doesn't know. I don't know how involved you are in her life or why September didn't have a support group and ended up checking herself in."

"First of all, even new moms with excellent family support can experience PPD severe enough to need round-the-clock care. I had your dad and both grandmas when I had PPD after the twins were born. Second, I can't share details September doesn't approve. But know there was a plan, and things should have been covered while I was in Florida. But I don't see her daily. I was not aware the baby blues had grown into something more until I got Jethro's call about the baby in the office. I couldn't tell him anything, either. September asked me not to."

"Which brings me back to my point. It doesn't matter what I ask. You won't tell me what I want to know." Sometime during his twenties, Adam realized his mother had mastered the art of disseminating only the things she wanted to, especially when it came to confidences.

"It depends on what you want to know. Some things September needs to tell. You understand how the client-confidentiality thing works."

This conversation had more circles than I-90 had exit ramps. "Why can't I read Sven's file?"

His mother didn't answer for a moment. "If I don't answer the question, then your mind will probably find an answer or worse." She took a deep breath before continuing. "I believe Sven Bent is Harmony's father, and I have been monitoring him. That stays between us."

Believe as in don't know for sure? Or carefully worded? Neither question would garner a usable answer. "Why would she choose me to take care of Harmony?"

"I have my suspicions, and I am sure you do too, but September is the only one with the answer. Although had I been in town, you might not be involved at all."

"You mean she wouldn't have checked into the hospital?" He turned into his parents' subdivision.

"No, I don't think my presence would have lessened the depression, but I may have gotten her into help earlier on an out-patient basis. Her housekeeper monitored things but got strep last week, and then her child caught it. She didn't dare be around the baby. Grandma breaking her hip added to everything else going on in September's life, it was a perfect storm."

"Are you going to tell me anything about what is going on or just hint at it and leave me wondering?" Adam parked in the driveway.

Melanie opened her door. "Let me talk to September, and then I will fill you in on what I can."

Adam beat her to the back to get her suitcase. "When do you think you will get to see her?"

"Dr. Brooks asked me to call when I got into town. September put me down as her emergency contact and signed a HIPAA waiver." Melanie held open the front door.

Adam stopped at the first stair and looked up at his mother. "How involved are you in September's life?"

"We've talked weekly for years, other than a couple weeks here and there over the past year."

Grabbing the suitcase by the handle, Adam carried it into the house. Chances were his mother knew more about their breakup, or whatever it was, than he did.

It wasn't a smile, at least not according to the parenting books, but it looked like one. September smiled back at her baby and stuck out her tongue. A few short seconds later Harmony forced her tongue out of her mouth. The nurse told her the mimicking response wouldn't last for long, so have fun with it now. September opened her mouth wide. Harmony tried but ended hers with a yawn. The clock counted down the minutes until Adam and Melanie would arrive. How much would Melanie tell Adam? Under normal circumstances, she kept secrets better than a bank vault. However, this week resembled anything but normal.

A nurse in princess scrubs entered. "Rayne? Security called. Your visitors are here. Do you need any help with Harmony?"

September moved Harmony from her lap to her arms. "No, I changed her a few moments ago."

The nurse followed her down the hall to the visitors' room. Through the window, she saw Melanie sitting, ankles crossed, relaxed as always. The relaxed *pose*. A sham, experience had taught her. Like all the Hastings, she was always on alert. Adam stood near one corner, like a tiger ready to spring. The nurse used her card to open the door, September entered, and the door shut behind her.

Melanie stood immediately. "How are you, sweetheart, and how is my little elf girl?" Melanie hugged them both.

September transferred Harmony to the arms of her stand-in grandmother. "She's been a perfect baby today. Eat, sleep, poop, repeat."

Melanie laughed. Adam smiled and relaxed at the joke.

"We need to talk. Don't worry. They don't record in here without permission. They only recorded our first meeting to evaluate." September sat on the edge of the chair, using all the words she'd planned. "Adam, please sit. I am sure your mother didn't tell you much since I officially hired her last July. I also know I am not yet quite thinking straight. I worry they will take Harmony away or that I won't be a good mother. The dark cloud in my life is something I can't see through. What I am trying to say is I doubt my judgment, so, Melanie, I give you permission to tell Adam anything you need to about the last six months. Though, Adam, it won't be everything you want to know because I am not ready to discuss the six months between the time I used Hastings Security and when I hired Melanie. If there is something he needs to know to protect Harmony, tell him." September looked at her hands. If any silent communication passed between the other people in the room, she didn't want to know.

Adam took the seat nearest her on the couch. "What I want to know is why choose me?"

Three little words for such an enormous question. Melanie continued to bounce Harmony in her arms as she walked to the farthest corner of the tiny room. Not that it gave them any real privacy. The question had multiple answers, and like a college midterm, more than one answer could be right, and most fit under certain circumstances. "I needed Harmony to be safe. After I met with my ob-gyn, she told me she was concerned and gave me the number for the hospital. I looked it up. At the time, I thought from the description, *This isn't me. I am not that depressed.*" September waved her hand in front of her face, trying to clear away the unimportant detail. "I read they did family therapy, and I thought about family, and you came to mind. Later that night, when I started to cross—" She couldn't talk about those moments she'd come close to ending everything. "I asked myself 'What would Melanie do?' and I thought of you. You acting as Harmony's dad seemed so right. Then it sounded crazy, especially when I left her at the office door, but I did wait to make sure your secretary found her. She isn't trained as a bodyguard, is she?"

"What makes you say that?" asked Adam.

"There is no way I would have stayed hidden from any of you. She didn't look around— just unlocked the door and took Harmony into the office."

"Elle is new and still learning. However, unexpected babies aren't in the handbook. I am glad you waited to make sure Harmony was safe."

The secretary was young, single, and pretty but not overdone. September had watched the Hasting brothers long enough to know their type. "Which one of you is dating her?"

"What?" Melanie turned from the corner. She must be listening closer than she appeared to be.

Adam shook his head. "No one is dating her. She is a former client, now an employee."

"Sorry, I don't know where my head went. I'm totally out of line."

Melanie came closer. "Oh, you are talking about Elle. I told you about her. She is the woman Alan guarded in the big name mix-up mess last fall."

The one Alan has a crush on but won't act on it because he rescued her. September had understood the unspoken message in one of Melanie's rants about her sons being dense when it came to women. September nodded and moved her focus back to Adam. "Dr. Brooks asked if you were the real father and if you would take part in family therapy."

"What did you tell her?"

"I gave an evasive answer on the first question and said I didn't know if you would participate. It isn't like we are, or were, or even could be—" She felt the heat rise in her face. She hated to be flustered in front of him.

Adam didn't speak. September stilled her hands in her lap and waited. *What a stupid question.*

"Can I give you an answer in the morning?" He angled his head so he could look her in the eye. "I want to talk to Mom and Dad and get their opinion. I don't want to make things more difficult for you in the long term."

The answer wasn't what she wanted but better than expected. "Tomorrow would be fine. Melanie, Dr. Brooks also asked if you would participate. You have been the closest thing I have had to a mother for years."

Melanie adjusted the sleeping baby in her arms. "I would be happy to take part. Although I feel it would be better to turn your security over to Hastings. Perhaps under the direction of one of the nonfamily members. That way we are not mixing business and family. Or if you are more comfortable, maybe Dermot Security. If I can trust Abbie to them, I can trust you to them."

Another set of eyes watching her every move. "I would like

my head of security to be female. And I trust you will share what you need to with whom you need to." *Please understand what I am saying.* September wasn't ready for Adam to learn everything. She wanted to share most of the story with him in private, later. Yet for everyone's safety some of her secrets needed to be disclosed before then.

"I'll talk to Jethro. There are a couple of excellent female guards I can recommend."

A tap came on the door, and a nurse appeared at the window, pointing to her watch.

Everyone stood without speaking. September touched Harmony's arm, her tears pooling. If Adam would hold Harmony, Melanie could give her a much-needed hug. But if September opened her mouth to orchestrate it, she wouldn't be able to keep her sobs at bay, so she stepped back and turned to Adam, hoping a half smile would do.

She was surprised when Adam opened his arms, the invitation clear. September stepped into them and let the tears fall. It was the hug she'd been wanting for more than a year.

AS THE TRAFFIC INCHED ALONG, Adam wondered if there was a basketball game tonight. A Bulls game could impact driving in the area. He stopped at another light.

His mother spoke for the first time since they'd left the hospital fifteen minutes ago. "I'll have Alan send over the file you wanted to read. Sven acted as the head of September's security for a few months. Without going into detail, that man is not the type of bodyguard Hastings would hire."

In Adam's experience, only two types of people went into the security business—those who felt a need to protect others from harm and those who wanted license to harm others in the name of doing good. In school, they were the bullies. As adults, they enjoyed being able to tell people to back off and give them a shove, necessary or not. It was often hard to determine which was which from a résumé or meeting them the first time. Backgrounds could be the same—former military or law enforcement. It wasn't until you saw them in action that the bully was discerned from the hero. Over the years, his father had hired a few guards he'd had to let go when they crossed the line from bodyguard to bully. "She wouldn't have been prepared for a bodyguard who didn't meet father's code of conduct."

"She wasn't."

Adam pulled into a parking lot and shut off the SUV so he could focus on the conversation. "Did he hurt her?"

Melanie looked out the window. "I'm not sure how to answer. I will disclose that he is the threat I am concerned about most in her life."

"Because he is Harmony's father or something else?"

"I can't confirm your assumption." His mother turned to face him.

"September released you from some confidentiality when she said you could turn over your security to dad."

"Yes, but that information does not include who is the father. Only whom I consider to be current threats to September and Harmony. And, yes, Sven is not someone I want in her vicinity. I also don't want Shyla around September without a third party in the room. That will be more difficult with someone else as head of security. "

"I never liked Shyla."

"Shyla is a marketing genius. And she cares for September enough to keep her out of harm's way, for the most part. She isn't a bad woman. It is the rare manager who cares for her client more than she does the money."

"Shyla never liked having me around."

"Of course not. For September, being married would change everything with her career. You were a threat."

Adam opened his mouth, ready to correct his mother, but she put up her hand.

"I should have told your father to rotate you out of September's security team the summer before you quit. The two of you danced around each other for months, both in denial of your feelings. I didn't pull you because I thought you were both half in love, and I didn't see it ending with you walking away."

"I didn't—" Adam stopped talking when Mom started to frown. "I did what I thought was best. She could have been killed. I wasn't paying enough attention to her surroundings and too much to September."

"You could have quit being her bodyguard without quitting her life."

There wasn't a good answer short of admitting that his mother was right. He hadn't seen it then. Now it was too late.

In the back seat, Harmony started to fuss. Adam started the car and hoped she would fall back asleep.

September sat up in bed, hand over her mouth. Had she screamed? She listened for the footsteps of a nurse or attendant. None came. According to the clock, it wasn't yet midnight. She lay back on the bed. Better to acknowledge the nightmare than to pretend it didn't happen. A secured wing of the hospital protected her. Harmony was safely asleep at the Hastings'. Only a complete idiot would attempt to get to Harmony there. Although she hadn't seen any media in the past two days, if a story broke about her location or Harmony's existence, she would have learned of it from Dr. Brooks.

Fluffing the impossibly flat pillow, she thought about the comments she'd heard in the various classes and counseling sessions. So many of them focused on honesty. Her career image had been built on her reputation for honesty and chastity. Ironically, had she been truthful with Adam and herself last year when he'd kissed her, things might be different now. Her choices leading to the conception of Harmony would never have been made, or perhaps she would be married now and Harmony really would have Adam for a father. Dr. Brooks would want her to talk about things from her past. Some of the hurts were obvious to the world—orphaned at fifteen, growing up on stage, and the very existence of Harmony proving she broke promises to God and her fans. During the last six months, she had faced much of those talking to Melanie and writing in a journal in secret code. Perhaps she was paranoid, but if her thoughts and feelings were ever made public—she shuddered. She hoped her code was indecipherable. The learning was in the writing, not so much in the reading, and so she often wrote sentences using the first letter of each word. "*Melanie asked me if I still loved Adam,*" became "MamiIslA." She defied any cryptographer to figure out the meaning when thrown in the middle of her coded pages. For fun, she would write random paragraphs in French, some in code and others not.

Sleep wouldn't come. She turned on one of her lights and picked up the journal she'd received in class earlier that day. Since it contained assignments, she hadn't coded most of the pages. September opened to the fifth to the last page.

InttAwh. I need to tell Adam what happened.

WhbInslh? Will he believe I never stopped loving him?

IunwIwd. I understand now what I was doing.

Itmmhonbpmiar. I think my manager helped, or not, by pushing me into another relationship.

Icbhfcim. I can't blame her for choices I made.

IbtIhtmsel. I bought the lie he told me sex equals love.

ItawIcumethmfiohtwtfoah? Is there a way I can use my experience to help my fans instead of hurting them when they find out about Harmony?

The last sentence made her stop. She'd written it out nearly substituting the word *friends* for *fans*. As Shyla feared, she would lose fans over giving her virtue away to someone she shouldn't have, but was there a way to turn the experience to good? Who could she ask?

Adam. For five years he had been the voice of reason keeping her feet on the ground when an award or accolade had her floating ten feet off the ground, reminding her that charity done without the media's presence was usually more powerful than when the camera was around to record it. His advice, though not always wanted, always proved correct. More than once his suggestions rounded out the lyrics to a song she was writing or caused her to take a second look at a contract or invitation. Even though she hadn't agreed at the time, his choice to quit had been for her too. If she had told the truth …

Never look back, or you'll miss where you're goin'.

Lyrics from one of her most popular songs rang through her mind.

I'm gonna be strong!
I'm gonna live right!
I'm gonna shun wrong!
I'll follow His light!
I'm gonna, I'm gonna, I'm gonna forward to home!

The song needed another verse about forgiveness and repentance. Looking back was only useful if it could help repair the future.

Tmlagtthe! This morning I am going to tell him everything!

THE 5:00 A.M. CALL WOULDN'T normally have awoken Adam since he would be at the gym. However, the 2:00 a.m. feeding had lasted almost two hours since Harmony decided it was time to play. She'd batted the bottle away and blown bubbles with the formula in her mouth. She would smile at him, then do it again after he smiled back. In his half-asleep imagination, it felt as if she were trying to talk to him and tell him wondrous things he couldn't understand. Harmony kicked her feet and waved her arms when he talked to her. A wiser man might not have encouraged her playfulness, missing the most magical of hours.

"Hello?"

"Please tell me you are not sick too." Alex's voice squeaked.

"No, I slept in. You sound terrible."

"Thanks, bro. I need you to fill in for me. Mrs. Crawford was asked to fill in for the speaker at one of those fund-raiser luncheons. She isn't taking the baby, but Mrs. Ogilvy will be there, so Andrew is already on duty. Since Mrs. Ogilvy's TedTalk, she has picked up unwanted attention, so he doesn't want to spread his team thin covering both women, and you know how their husbands are." Alex's rambling confirmed he was ill.

"I thought I was working with you for Mr. Crawford and Mr. Ogilvy." Adam got out of bed and stretched.

"Change of plans. I put another team on the misters. The threat is more critical to the wives."

"Will Abbie be at the lunch?"

"I think so, but we aren't sharing any info with her. She gives her own team enough fits."

Adam pulled the blanket up over his bed. Not his mother's standards, but it was made. "She stopped carrying a gun."

"Ugh." The grunt answered it all. Alex's twin had been carrying as long as the rest of them. "I can't believe it. Maybe now Simon Dermot can stop complaining to Dad."

"What time am I needed?"

"Sweep starts at oh-eight-hundred."

"I'll see if I can get Mom to take Harmony out to September."

"Thanks. I'll assume she can unless I hear otherwise. I'm going back to bed."

"Bye, Alex." The call disconnected before he finished speaking.

He found his parents in the kitchen dressed in their workout clothes. They stopped talking when he entered. Adam filled a glass with water and sat at the table with them. "Not even asking what I interrupted. Alex called. He's sick and asked me to cover for him with Mrs. Crawford. Can you take Harmony to September this morning?"

Mom stirred her lemon water. "What does he have?"

"No clue, but he sounds terrible."

"I can take Harmony, but do me a favor and write your report on Harmony for September." She finished her water. "I'll be back by seven."

His father stood. "Drop by the office after you're finished. I'll know how long we will need to cover for Alex by then and can work something out. Also, I am thinking Deidre for September's security lead. Any thoughts?"

Deidre Ross had joined the Hastings team last year. Hyperfocused the few times he worked with her, she'd been more than competent. "It would probably work. I've noticed she avoids shifts when the Crawford baby is in the mix. Not sure if that will work with Harmony."

"I'll ask her about that. I'd better catch up with your mother. It is only Valentine's Day and already she has twenty-one miles on me."

"I am sure you have her in reps."

Adam smiled as the back door shut. His parents had been "competing" at the gym as long as he could remember. His mother always finished the year with three hundred to five hundred more miles than his father, who usually ended the year with more reps at a higher weight. The winner of each competition received a week's vacation at the destination of their choice. The loser paid for it. So far it had worked out well for both parents.

The sounds of Harmony waking up came from the monitor. Adam hurried to change and feed her so he could do the same for himself. Halfway through the bottle, he remembered the note. He tried to balance a notepad on the arm of the chair so he could write, but a kick from Harmony sent the pad flying to the floor. He tried again with the same result. He hoped he would have time to write the note and take a shower, providing he got Harmony back to sleep so he could take one. He checked the time on his phone. Yikes, he would be late as it was. Forget the letter. He put the phone in selfie mode and pressed the record button.

"Good morning. Sorry I can't be there today. Harmony and I had fun last night. I shouldn't have played with her, but…" Phones were not allowed past security, but Mom would figure out a way to show September the video. He emailed the file and burped the baby.

"Okay, little one, how do I take a shower with you awake?" He pondered the situation, but nothing came to him. Maybe he could lay her on the floor outside his bathroom. On the way upstairs, he passed the pile of things his sister had brought. A pink-and-turquoise bouncy-chair thing that looked like a more comfortable version of the car seat sat on the floor. He grabbed it with his free hand and rushed up the stairs.

"Oh, look. It has a mobile." Adam fastened Harmony into the seat, turned the switch to on, and turned the seat away from the shower door. "Sorry, no watching men shower for, like, fifty years, little girl."

He had just lathered his hair with shampoo when the music stopped and Harmony began to fuss. As he started to rinse, her crying intensified. Adam shut off the shower with soap still in his hair and grabbed a towel. "Hey, pumpkin, what's wrong?" The second step out of the shower brought him to his knees as his dripping wet foot connected with a worn spot in the old linoleum. At his fall, Harmony cried louder. Adam crawled across the floor and turned her seat around. Instantly she stopped and gave him a little smile. "Fine. You can sit facing the bathroom. Just no peeking. I don't want to have to explain anything to your mom."

Adam concluded the shortest shower he'd taken since leaving the army. Harmony bounced and kicked in the seat while he dried himself in the shower. This time he took more care stepping out. As soon as he walked into his closet, she started fussing again. Adam turned the seat so it faced the bedroom. "You don't like having people do things behind your back, do you? If I keep talking while I am out of sight, can we finish? I'd rather not dress in front of a lady." He pulled on his pants as fast as he could to the sounds of fussing but figured he could go shirtless. That wouldn't scar her for life, would it? He turned the seat around while he finished dressing.

He heard his mother in the hallway as he worked the last button.

She knocked on the open door. "You're buttoned crooked."

Adam looked down and started to rebutton his shirt. "How did you do it, Mom? All I wanted was a quick shower, and I could hardly get it done!"

Laughter filled the room as Melanie bent down and removed Harmony from the seat. "There were days I couldn't get a shower at all until your father got home. If I put the twins in the playpen, then either you or Alan would start a fight. If the two of you were watching TV, then the twins were screaming. I think I gave up with Andrew. Half the showers I took I brought him in with me and prayed the four of you wouldn't set off the smoke alarms."

"It is a wonder every mother in the world doesn't have PPD from lack of sleep alone."

"I think most women get at least a little, what, when you add in the changing hormones from concluding a pregnancy to the odd sleep hours. It is hard for a body to cope." Melanie walked to the door with Harmony.

"Thanks, Mom."

"Oh, I love spending time with this angel."

"No, I mean thanks for having all of us five kids. Thanks for raising us."

"You're welcome."

Adam pulled on his shoes and socks and rushed to his vehicle, hoping he wouldn't be too late. Never again would he think of a mother's job as easy.

The lunch noise in the cafeteria rose as patients from several units converged on the room. September sat at a table with several other moms from her ward. She noticed most of the other tables comprised similar groupings. In the corner, a group of twenty-somethings conversed over heart-shaped cookies with pink frosting. A few men in their fifties sat at another table. Careful not to make eye contact with any other patients, she briefly bowed her head over her food. She didn't dare say a prayer out loud for fear of someone commenting. Orderlies patrolled the room, attempting to blend in, paying particular attention to the plastic utensils. For institutional fare, the food was better than expected.

Two young women rose from the corner table and wound their way through the dining room to the area where the PPD moms sat.

"Excuse me." The one with spiky blonde hair tapped September on the shoulder. "Has anyone ever told you that you could be September Platt's doppelgänger?"

"September who?"

"The singer. She sings Christian-pop stuff." The short brunette tilted her head and squinted. "You could totally be her body double if you lost about twenty pounds and cut your hair."

"Oh." September took a bite of her burger, hoping they would take the hint and leave.

Across the table, Leisha joined in. "Rayne, I see it. Not huge, but there is a resemblance."

One of the orderlies passed by. "Is there a problem, ladies?"

The blonde pointed at September. "Nah, we were commenting on how much she looked like the singer September."

The orderly shook his head. "Maybe, but she is trying to eat. Why don't you two move along?"

Madison rolled her eyes. "I get told I look like Grace Kelly all the time. Some people have those faces."

"I once read that everyone has seven people in the world who look like them but that the chances of meeting even one of them are infinitesimal," said the woman on her other side.

September hurried through the rest of her food. "I'll see you all back up there. I want to check on Harmony."

Dr. Brooks waited for the elevator. "Did they ever get that video Adam sent to play for you?"

"Yes, one nurse put it on her tablet." September massaged her palm with her thumb while she waited.

No one else joined them in the elevator. The doctor lowered her gaze to September's hands. "Is everything all right?"

"Not sure. Two women from a different ward came over to our

table and told me how much I looked like the singer—"

"You are looking better than when you first got here. Perhaps it would be better if you ate up in the ward. I think in your case, socialization might not be the best thing."

"Thank you."

The elevator pinged as the doors opened.

"Doctor, one more thing. Adam said he is coming to family therapy tonight. Could I ask that he come a little earlier? I would like to talk to him alone for a few minutes. I was going to tell him some things he needs to know this morning, but since he couldn't come..."

"We try to give all the partners time together both before and after the sessions, so that shouldn't be a problem. Let's check the schedule. You may not need to have him come early at all." Dr. Brooks stopped at the nurses' station and retrieved her tablet. "Will a half hour be long enough? That is what I built into the appointment for you."

"That should be fine." September left the doctor and went in search of Harmony. She glanced at the clock above the nursery. Four hours and fifteen minutes from now she would make the speech she had prepared last night. If she didn't chicken out.

ADAM CHECKED HIS WATCH AS the traffic light a block south of the hospital turned red. He had ten minutes to spare. Mom told him September looked disappointed he couldn't come and even more disappointed when the video he sent wouldn't stream to the TV so she could watch it since cell phones were not allowed on the floor—a point he shouldn't have overlooked. At the hospital, he went through the routine of emptying his pockets and leaving his keys at the desk. The orderly led him to a room smaller than the one they'd exchanged Harmony in. He waited only a second before September came in alone.

She stood awkwardly by the door. The only seating in the room was the sofa. Adam scrunched to one side, leaving as much room as possible for September. "As bad as a blind date? I don't bite." He patted the space next to him.

September sat down and pulled a paper out of her pocket. "I wrote everything I need to say. Please let me get to the end before we discuss anything."

Adam nodded and looked at the paper. If he could read the page, then this might go faster, but all he could see was gibberish.

"I need you to understand I am not blaming you for any of the choices I made. Perhaps if I hadn't lied the morning after our kiss, things might be different now. I thought if you believed the kiss hadn't affected me, you wouldn't leave." She paused, and Adam opened his mouth to argue, but she shook her head. "In the days after you left, I told myself it was for the best. You had some valid reasons. Shyla wouldn't let me go after you. I tried to call once, but you didn't pick up."

What if he had picked up? Adam had held the phone, debating, until her photo had faded from the screen. She hadn't left a message, and he'd called her back a dozen times, but her demanding schedule always sent him to voicemail.

"Shyla hired a new firm. At first they were professional. I never noticed them. One day, I think we were in Montreal, a new guard joined them. He would talk to me. I didn't realize it at the time, but he was the kind of guy you'd warned me about—the kind who saw me as a challenge."

Adam tried not to wince. The more Shyla used September's choice to remain chaste until marriage as a marketing tool, the more fan letters September received with offers to be the one to initiate her into the real world. Many of the letters were obscenely detailed. They never made it to September's attention. They'd flagged a few as potential stalkers when they also posted to social media repeatedly. Adam had argued more than once with Shyla about her tactics and tried to caution September about some of her dates who were known players in the music industry. He thought she had learned her lesson when he'd had to intervene on a few dates.

"Looking back, I realize I was trying to fill a void in my life I didn't understand existed. Often this guard got himself assigned to do the sweep of my hotel room at night and we would talk. I discovered later he was the head of my team. I thought we were friends. One night he kissed me. It wasn't as fulfilling as ours had been, but still, it filled part of the emptiness inside. Over the next few weeks, we continued to talk and flirt. I was looking for something and kept hoping he would answer my need. The night

Harmony was conceived, he didn't force me. For him, it consummated a month of seduction. He'd won a game I didn't know I was playing. Even as it happened, I knew what I felt was fake. Not even cubic zirconia fake. More like the old-fashioned paste jewels—mere glass wrapped in foil. Unlike the movies, the experience left me feeling emptier than before. Having conquered me, he became possessive and controlling, demanding more, which I refused to give him. When I asked to have him removed from the detail, he threatened to go to the tabloids. I paid him off under the condition he never touch me again."

Adam struggled to remain focused on the story. He wanted to pound the man. Although she hadn't said the name, he assumed it was Sven. The timeline fit with when he'd started adding money to his bank account. Alan's dossier included many payments leading up to the big one.

"Weeks later I realized our one night could not remain a secret forever. I asked him if we could talk." September closed her eyes and took a deep breath. "He made it very clear he did not want to be a father. Shyla found out. I am sure you can imagine her reaction. She canceled my performance, claiming I was ill."

"The one in Dallas?" Adam couldn't help asking. Dallas was the only performance she'd missed before the end of the tour and going into "rehab."

"Yes. Please let me finish?" Her voice shook, and she clutched the paper, her tears threatening to spill over, but he didn't dare touch her. "Shyla's solution was termination. I refused. You know how she can be, so you will understand why, after several days, I agreed but told her not until the tour ended, as we only had three more weeks. She discreetly found a doctor in Seattle, and I had her schedule an appointment for three days after the tour concluded. The guard threatened to go to the tabloids again, only this time Shyla intervened." September bit her lip. He'd seen her do that before when she left out details, choosing which words wouldn't be a lie. "They came to a mutually beneficial agreement."

Adam kept silent but only with great effort. The agreement must have been what allowed Sven to start his own company. They must have paid him double what they thought the story would be worth to the tabloids. The word *if* kept floating across his mind. It didn't seem like September was blaming him, but she should. He'd left her. He should have known she'd lied when she said she didn't care for him and that the kiss was only another kiss from a fan who wanted a piece of her.

"Shyla insisted on going to Seattle with me, along with two bodyguards, neither one him. I kept the burner phone you gave me for emergencies. Shyla monitored my every move. She knew too much."

Adam nodded. On occasion, they would find cameras or listening devices, usually when September had a date. Andrew could never figure out where they were coming from. They'd never thought it could be the same person in so many places. He cursed himself for missing the obvious.

"I called Melanie to get her help. Your mother advised me to have morning sickness more often than I felt it and to wear a Cub's cap on the plane. By the time I got off at Sea-Tac airport, neither Shyla nor the bodyguards would follow me into the women's room, and they had given up forcing me to wait for one of the private family bathrooms. Unfortunately, I didn't have to fake much. I felt like my baby was trying to help in the plan to let her live. Your mom disguised me as a very pregnant woman to get me out of the airport. We walked right past Shyla. She didn't even look twice." September folded the paper and looked at him.

"Mom has a talent for disguises. I'm glad she could help you when I couldn't. For the record, I said and did things the morning after our kiss I regret too. I wish—"

September held up her hand. "This is one of those times where we can't look back."

"Never look back, or you'll miss where you're goin'?" Adam didn't sing the words. "Where is it we are going?"

"I don't know. But I like the sound of 'we.' Can we go there together?"

Adam took her hand in his. It was smaller than he remembered. "If I could have one do-over in life, it would be the following morning and leaving. This might not be the best time to start a relationship, though."

September shook her head. "We aren't starting, we are redirecting. The PPD isn't permanent, and I shouldn't make any major life choices while I am recovering. But having you in my life is a choice I made long before now. I think I can trust it."

A knock sounded at the door, and the orderly stuck her head in. "Dr. Brooks is ready for you now."

He didn't let go of her hand as they walked down the hall or into the room where Dr. Brooks held couples therapy. The doctor smiled at them as they sat down on the sofa together, passing the two chairs would make an obvious second choice.

"As a doctor, I try not to assume anything, so I will ask, what is the status of your relationship?"

September looked to Adam, and when his eyes met hers, his mouth turned up at the edges. He gave her hand a squeeze, and she said, "I am not quite sure, but we've decided to move forward together."

"Sep—Rayne and I spent a lot of time together over the last five years. We've been good friends and more than friends. I think we are better together."

Dr. Brooks nodded. "Then, with a few exceptions, I will treat the two of you as if you are in a long-term, committed relationship."

The half-hour session flew by. Perhaps it only seemed short because Adam was holding her hand. Dr. Brooks detailed the need for support after September's release. Adam said he had already discussed this with his parents and suggested September and Harmony move in with them.

The doctor looked at her watch. "Rayne, your dinner is being brought up. Adam, you are welcome to stay during dinner and while September feeds Harmony. I can't have a meal brought up, but there are snacks at the nurses' station you could pilfer."

"Thank you. I think I will stay."

The orderly took them back to the little room they first met in. September pushed the lasagna around her plate while Adam ate a cracker.

"Do I need to leave so you can eat?"

"I feel odd eating while you don't."

"Pretend I am your bodyguard. Do you know how many dinners you ate while I watched?"

September felt the heat rise in her face and took a bite, hoping to mask her discomfort.

A nurse knocked on the door before opening it. "This little one is awake, freshly changed, and ready to see her parents."

Adam crossed the room and took Harmony from the nurse. September pushed the tray to the side and held out her arms.

"Finish eating. I can entertain the little princess while you eat." He sat down and turned his full attention to her daughter. "I need to apologize for not bringing you flowers or chocolates for Valentine's Day."

"If they hadn't served us heart cookies at lunch, I might not have even known. I didn't get you anything either." The next bite refused to go down. If only she had made other choices and Adam was Harmony's real father. Most likely she would still have PPD, but so much of the stress she felt wouldn't exist. She forced her attention back to her food. Eating wasn't optional for nursing mothers. After a few more bites, she took a deep breath. There were still things she needed to say.

"His name is Sven. I think your mother has a file on him."

"She gave it to me. Did you know he had a record?"

With her mouth full of lightly seasoned garlic bread, she could only nod. "Shyla knew. I found out when they made their deal."

"How much do you know about their deal?" His voice was higher than normal and singsongy as he addressed the question more to Harmony.

"As little as possible. They both assumed I would take care of things. But I never signed that I would end Harmony's life. I didn't sign the contract at all." There was more to the incident, but it would be enough to let him know to guard against Sven and Shyla, who were threats in different ways.

Adam stood and was rocking Harmony in his arms when he spoke again, his voice back to normal. When she looked up, she realized he'd positioned himself between the window at the side of the door and her.

"Did Sven ever hit you?"

The question was too specific for her to dodge. She nodded.

"Do you believe he would hurt you again?"

Not wanting to see his reaction, September closed her eyes before nodding.

"Would he hurt Harmony?"

September looked at her angel daughter. "He might." *He tried to kill her once. He tried to kill us both. How do I explain that?*

Adam stood still until Harmony started fussing. September wondered for a moment if she had spoken her thoughts out loud. "I see. You finish eating. This little angel will not wait much longer."

September shoved the last few bites in her mouth and tried to swallow. "Will you put the tray outside? I think it makes them nervous to have any of us with a fork and knife for too long."

He traded Harmony for the tray. He didn't even have the door open before the orderly took it from him and checked the utensils. "I see you were not exaggerating about their obsession over forks and knives."

"Even if I am not a danger to myself, which I no longer feel I am, a misplaced fork or knife could be found by someone else. They don't even allow us to keep our toothbrushes."

Adam perched himself on the arm of the couch, giving her ample room to feed Harmony. He no longer blushed when she nursed.

"That sounds like a reasonable precaution."

She thought he might say more, but he didn't.

"I want to live. I am not in the same place I was when I came here. If that was the blackest night, then this is the time before sunrise on a cloudy day. Each moment is a bit brighter. I know there are still clouds to deal with, but in the light, they are less ominous. Does that make any sense?"

"Some. I didn't experience PTSD like some of my fellow soldiers, but I watched enough friends to know when they started feeling hope that things could get better. I see the same hope in you."

Not wanting him to see the gathering tears, she turned her attention to burping Harmony before she was ready for it.

When she failed to produce results, Adam took the baby from her. "Here, little one, let's show Mama how big you can burp." He almost instantly garnered a loud burp. "The problem is Mama doesn't have huge hands." His teasing put September at ease.

Like they'd discussed in morning group, she wasn't deficient. Sometimes there were things they should ask for help with. "And Mama would look hilarious with hands as big as yours."

Laughter filled the room, and the clouds in her mind shifted, allowing more hope in.

FRIDAY MORNING, DR. BROOKS STOPPED Adam in the hallway after he dropped Harmony off. "Do you have a moment?"

Adam followed her into a formal doctor's office—the kind with leather chairs around a polished desk and framed diplomas on the wall.

"Rayne signed a release for me to talk with you. Monday is President's Day, so I won't be here for the next three days, but I will be a phone call away. I've been debating about releasing her before I leave. She is in the gray area, which means she could go either way. Her response to her medication has been excellent, and when I talk to her, she is doing better. However, I think she would benefit from a couple more days of respite and more parenting classes, as well as therapy. Rayne's case is complicated because of who she is. She had a close call in the cafeteria, and I've had her eat up here since. There are now a few staff members who believe she is a famous singer." Dr. Brooks tapped her pen on her desk and smiled. "Most of the staff working here over the weekend aren't here during the week, and because of the three-day weekend, there are several temps on duty, starting today. I am afraid not all the temps will keep her identity safe. With what little details she has shared about her life and what I know from her public profile, I think a leak about her location and reason for being here would be more harmful than leaving too early."

"What does Rayne think?"

"I haven't talked to her yet. I need to know if you and your parents are ready to care for her. Your mother had PPD and thinks she knows what to watch for, some of the things we discussed in last night's counseling."

"Abrupt mood changes, not caring for herself or Harmony?"

"That and one of the possible side effects of the antidepressant meds she is taking is suicidal thoughts."

"Is that some terrible irony?"

"Sadly, it is one of those two-edged swords, but the cure is worth the minimal risk. If you feel you are ready, I'll release her tonight and give you my on-call number. Then, on Tuesday, I'd like you both to come in at nine in the morning so I can do a follow-up evaluation. I refer patients back to their ob-gyns or a more local doctor to follow up and find counseling. However, Rayne is who she is, and the fewer people in the city who know, the better."

"Is there anything I need to bring for her release?"

"Did you bring up her personal clothing already?"

"My mother did."

"Then make sure she has a coat. I'll see you for your regular appointment at five."

Adam waited until he was sitting in the car to call his mother, then he headed to the office. He wouldn't be working this weekend after all.

Am I ready? Can I leave and be normal-ish?

The questions repeated themselves in her mind a hundred times before lunch. She nursed Harmony as the other women made their way down to the cafeteria. Twenty minutes later, her daughter fell asleep, and her lunch tray had yet to arrive, so she took her sleeping daughter to the nursery, laid her in her assigned crib, and talked with one of the caregivers. A new woman sat behind the reception desk.

"Pardon me, my lunch tray didn't come up today."

"I didn't order any. What is your name?"

"Rayne."

The woman shuffled papers. "Oh, here is the order." She checked her computer. "It is too late for me to have it delivered, but I see you are cleared to go to the cafeteria. Why don't you go down there? You have thirty minutes left until the parenting class starts."

September could think of a dozen reasons why she didn't want to go down, but her stomach was rumbling. "Sure, I'll run down, but will you be sure to order up my dinner?"

"This isn't the Waldorf. Not everyone gets room service."

The comment took September a moment to process. It was the first rude thing she'd heard in days. "I am aware this isn't a hotel, but my family therapy time is at five, and I will not have time to go down."

"Oh. I didn't realize. I thought you got special treatment because you are some big music star."

A few choice words ran through September's head. She hoped she looked confused. "I'm just a mom like everyone else. I think you may be confused."

"Whatever. You'd better hurry."

September hurried to the cafeteria and picked up a sandwich, apple, cookie, and milk so she wouldn't need any utensils. After having her lunch checked twice by orderlies, she was allowed to return to her floor. She ate in her room, not wanting to experience another run-in with the receptionist.

Ready or not, Dr. Brooks was right. It was safest if she left.

Alan burst into Adam's office and thrust his tablet across the desk. "You've got trouble."

September--Bad Girl or Bad Mom?

The blurry photo showed a woman holding an infant over her shoulder. They were dressed exactly as September and Harmony had been when he'd dropped the baby off at the hospital that morning.

"The story broke in the last"—Alan checked his watch—"three minutes. So far it is only on a handful of not-so-reputable blogs. Since it violated HIPAA laws to get this photo, even the tabloids will double-check before picking this one up. But it won't stop fans from sharing on social media."

Adam grabbed his jacket. "Call Mom and ask Dad who he put on security. I am headed to the hospital now—see if I can beat the paparazzi."

Once in his SUV, he used the hands-free phone to call Dr. Brooks.

A receptionist answered.

"I need to speak with Dr. Brooks."

"She is in a meeting. May I take a message?"

"This is Mr. Adam. Please tell her there has been an emergency and I am coming to the hospital now. Have her call me ASAP." He rattled off his number before disconnecting.

A few minutes later, his mother called. "Give me twenty to get to the hospital. I am changing into something very uncomfortable and bringing more uncomfortable clothes." Good his mom was thinking more clearly than he was. They would need disguises.

Five minutes out, he gave the hospital a second call. The same receptionist answered.

"This is Mr. Adam. May I speak with Dr. Brooks?"

"She went into another meeting. May I help you?"

"Did you give her my message from twenty minutes ago?"

"I put it in the pile on her desk."

"This is an emergency. One of her patients is in danger. I need her to call me into security. I will be at the hospital in three minutes."

"Sir, it isn't visiting hours. You may not come until 6:30 p.m. unless you have special authorization."

"That is why I am calling. This is an emergency."

"Then I suggest you hang up and dial 911."

The line went dead. Adam tried to shelf his frustrations as he pulled into the lot. Four or five people milled about with cameras. Paparazzi. He hoped they were enjoying the below-freezing weather. He put his gun in the car safe. No point in making security more difficult than it needed to be.

He moderated his pace so as not to draw attention as he hurried into the building. He recognized both security officers at the check-in.

"Mr. Adam, we don't have you down for another two hours. I'm sorry, but you can't enter."

"I've been trying to call Dr. Brooks. There is an emergency involving one of her patients, but the receptionist won't pass my message on."

The older security guard looked him up and down. "You are one of Jethro's boys, aren't you?"

"You know my father?"

"Been wondering all week if you were one of his sons. Shouldn't ask. Is the patient a client?"

"Yes."

"Does this emergency have anything to do with the photographers gathering in the parking lot?"

"Yes, I believe so. Most of them are smart enough not to come in, but they are paparazzi or worse."

He turned to the other guard. "Call up Dr. Brooks' pager. And then get more security to move those people out to the street." He turned to Adam. "Let's get you processed. Anything else I need to know that won't violate privacy?"

Adam checked his watch. "My mother should be here soon. But she won't look like herself."

"She knows me. I think I can work that out." The older guard nodded.

The desk phone rang, and the younger guard answered. He handed the phone to Adam. "It's Dr. Brooks."

"Doctor, someone took a photo of one of your patients. There are already photographers hanging around the parking lot."

Dr. Brooks responded with what sounded like an expletive. "Hand the phone back to them and get up here."

The guards let him through.

SEPTEMBER LOOKED UP FROM HER journal when Dr. Brooks came back into the group-therapy room. "Ladies, I am sorry, but there is an emergency, and I cannot finish this session with you. So we don't interrupt the other groups on the floor, please stay here until our session is scheduled to be over. Would anyone like their baby brought in?"

Hands shot up and people talked all at once.

"Ladies, it looks like most of you want your children. Is there anyone who doesn't?"

One woman raised her hand. "If my daughter is sleeping, let her sleep. My husband said she had a difficult night."

Dr. Brooks turned to the nurse who had just come in. "Can you take care of this, please?" Another nurse entered, and Dr. Brooks exited the room. Nursery attendants came into the room with babies, one tapping September on the shoulder. "Will you please come with me?"

September gathered her journal and followed the attendant into the hall. Dr. Brooks stood at the reception desk, a phone between her shoulder and ear, flipping through the pages of a red binder. The attendant pointed to the doctor and left in the direction of the nursery. September stood near the desk, where she overheard Dr. Brooks. "Yes, code yellow. This breach isn't just about one person. No one will trust us...I don't know...Thank you."

The receptionist at the desk pulled a jacket and purse out of a drawer and stood. Dr. Brooks stepped in front of the half gate. "Where do you think you are going?"

"My shift ends at two."

"Perhaps you didn't understand my phone call to security. We are on a code-yellow lockdown. No one, including employees, in or out of the building. That includes you. Hey, is that a cell phone?" Dr. Brooks reached over the gate and pulled a phone from the pocket of the jacket. "There are no cell phones allowed in this part of the building."

"That is mine."

"Yes, and if you read the addendum you signed to work on this floor, it warned you that unauthorized electronics will be confiscated." The buzzer of the floor's entrance door interrupted what the doctor was going to say next. From where she stood, September could see the monitor showing Adam on the other side of the door. What was he doing here? Lockdown. Hastings Security. September's heart raced. Harmony!

Dr. Brooks dropped an arm around September and glared at the receptionist. "Buzz him in. And read the yellow section of this notebook. You are not to leave until cleared by myself and security."

"My phone?"

Dr. Brooks ignored the receptionist's question as she propelled September to one of the private meeting rooms. "Mr. Adam, in here please."

Adam shut the door behind them. "My mother should be coming. I asked security to send her up. But she may be in disguise. I tried to call—"

"There is a temp at the desk today. In fact, I may have found the culprit." Dr. Brooks pulled the phone out of her pocket. "Do you have a copy of the leaked photo?"

Adam pulled his own phone out of his pocket. "Security let me keep it." He tapped the front and handed it to Dr. Brooks.

September looked over the doctor's shoulder at the phone's screen. "That's me. How?" Adam wrapped his arm around her waist and pulled her close. She leaned into his side and felt his calming protection seep into her. "Hey, we got this. We'll keep you and Harmony safe."

"Someone took the photo on this floor." Dr. Brooks handed the phone back.

"Finding the source of the photo will go a long way toward shutting things down. September, do you have any idea when this was shot?"

Her heart rate picked up again as she studied the photo. "I think it was before lunch. I went to go change her diaper. My face is scrunched up. I was telling her what a stinky girl she was. Can I go get her, please?"

"Yes, let's go get her now, and we can figure out where the 'photographer' stood." Adam stepped toward the door. Dr. Brooks put an arm out to stop him.

"You can't go wandering around out there. I'll go with Rayne. She can stand where she did when the photo was taken, and I can back up until I have the same view. It may give us more ideas. I am sure they took the photo from near the reception desk."

Adam frowned.

"Is the phone you took from the receptionist unlocked?" asked September.

Dr. Brooks pulled it out of her pocket and examined it. "No, that would be too easy."

"Try to be discreet out there." Adam held open the door.

September didn't want to be discreet. She crossed to the place where the hallway turned to go to the nursery and stood about where she was in the photo. Dr. Brooks consulted Adam's phone and moved a couple times before nodding her head. September did her best not to run to the nursery to get Harmony.

Dr. Brooks returned to the room first and handed Adam's phone back. "I think someone took it from the reception-desk area, but I am not sure."

"Right now, getting September and Harmony out of here without the paparazzi downstairs realizing it and squelching the rumor is the best we can do."

"I want to find the person responsible. People are leery of mental-health hospitals, and this type of thing leaked is not helpful." Dr. Brooks reached for her pager. "It's security. I'll be right back."

September came into the room with a sleeping Harmony in her arms. "Please tell me everything." She sat in the rocker in the corner.

Adam checked his phone. "So far it seems to be only the few disreputable websites. Alan hasn't sent me any other alerts, and the software he uses to check threats is much more powerful than a year ago." Colin Ogilvie's latest software design had other uses than keeping the billionaire and his friends safe.

"Dr. Brooks spoke with me this morning about my leaving. I am not sure. Would we keep the same plan of me going to your parents' house for a while, or does this change things?"

"It is one of the safer options. Nothing in the two-paragraph article links you to us." His parents' house looked like any other on the street but hid a security system designed by his father, as well as a safe room. It would be as safe as they could get her.

Dr. Brooks returned to the room. "Your mother is in my office. I didn't want to bring her onto the floor in case it is the receptionist. I don't need to give her another reason to wonder what is happening. Your mom has an idea for checking the receptionist's story, but she needs to use your phone. I think if you take it to her and also take Harmony, I'll tell the receptionist you came to pick Harmony up for a doctor's appointment."

September gasped.

Adam knelt in front of the rocker. "The idea is good. It lets me get Harmony out of here. I've kept her safe all week. I'll keep her safe now."

She pulled her daughter close and kissed her brow. "I know you will. I'm just—"

"Scared? I am a little too. I don't like it when plans have to be composed on the fly." He placed his hand on her shoulder, trying to reassure her. It had been a calculated risk to tell her he felt scared. He hoped realizing she was not the only person with fears might help her accept the current situation.

"You're scared? But you are always so strong."

"I have emotions too. I just keep going until I get out of tough situations." He added a reassuring smile to his arsenal and felt her shoulders relax.

She lifted Harmony and set her in his arms. "You will keep us both safe."

Adam adjusted Harmony so he held her in one arm, then reached up with his free hand to trace the side of September's face. "We'll see you later. Mom is here, so everything will work out." He left the room hoping his words would be true.

If he hadn't known it was his mother in Dr. Brooks' office, he might not have guessed. The person in the sweater could have been male or female. "Here is my phone. Why do you need it?"

"It is the same model as the receptionist's. I will show her the photo on what she thinks is her phone and see how she reacts." His mother pulled her hair out of her collar and made quick work of putting it in a bun. "Then I will go from there. Deidre has some of her team at the grocery store three blocks south. If you think you are being followed, go in and buy cornflakes. If not, continue on to the house. I'll bring September with me. Dr. Brooks will get the discharge papers taken care of." She gave him a side hug and beamed at the sleeping baby.

Adam returned to security. The older guard had Harmony's seat, blanket, and diaper bag ready. "We got the photographers off the street. Reminded them about HIPAA laws and told them if there was someone of interest in the building, they could face a lawsuit. One of them left. I think there are only two still hanging around. The temperature is dropping, so I think they'll give up soon."

"Thanks"—Adam checked the guard's name tag—"Dell. Have a good day."

After putting Harmony in her car seat, Adam scanned the parking lot. No one seemed very interested in him.

There was no need to stop at the grocery store, which was a good thing as Harmony woke up and informed anyone in range that she wanted out of the car as soon as possible.

September stood near the door, listening as Melanie spoke to the receptionist. She could see the receptionist's face blanch. The woman attempted to run, but Melanie had her before she made it to the door. Dr. Brooks opened the door to the outer hall, and Melanie escorted the woman out.

Dr. Brooks beckoned September over. "Why don't you go gather your things and stay in your room. I need to get your paperwork done and deal with some things, like lifting the code yellow before too many of the patients realize we've closed down the hospital."

"What will happen to her?"

"I am not sure if there can be criminal charges or not. But at least for now, security can hold her while administration figures out a course of action. They will deny you were here. I assume they will try to protect the reputation of the hospital, which should also help you."

"Thanks, Dr. Brooks, for everything. This isn't the way I pictured this ending, but I think I'll be okay." September hugged the doctor.

"You will be. Adam has my emergency number. I'll send a nurse for you when it is time to slip you out of here."

There wasn't much to gather other than her journal and the few clothes Melanie had brought over. September exchanged the hospital's nursing top for one of her own shirts.

A cafeteria worker knocked on September's door and entered with a tray.

"I don't need—" September stopped when she realized the worker was Melanie.

"Good, because I made shepherd's pie, and I would like to get home to eat it. How about it?" Melanie took the cover off the tray, revealing a blue uniform and hairnet. "We will leave through the employee entrance."

ADAM CHECKED THE CLOCK AGAIN as he paced the living room. According to his mother's text, September and Melanie had left the hospital twenty minutes ago. Adam debated about giving in and feeding Harmony a bottle, but he figured September would need to feed Harmony as badly as Harmony needed to eat when they got here. This was one of those moments where a pacifier would come in handy. He circled the couch and crossed in front of the window again. His mom's sedan pulled into the driveway and idled while the garage door opened.

"Look! Mama is here." Harmony tried stuffing her fist in her mouth. Adam crossed the room to the kitchen and opened the door to the garage. His mother and September laughed as they got out of the car.

At the sight and sound of her mother, Harmony let out a wail.

September rushed over and gathered Harmony from Adam's arms. "Poor baby. I bet you're starving."

"There's a rocking chair in the nursery upstairs. Adam will show you where it is." Adam's mother gathered several parcels from the back of the car and followed September into the house.

Adam turned on the light in the nursery. "Mom's been waiting for a grandchild and has had this room ready for years. Although it wasn't until Abbie's announcement two months ago that it started to take shape. Do you need anything?"

"Would you mind bringing me a water bottle? I seem to get thirsty when I nurse." September settled into the chair and tossed a blanket over her shoulder as Adam hurried down the stairs.

His mother passed him on the way. "Come back upstairs and talk to us as soon as you can."

When Adam returned, he found his mother scrolling through her tablet. "Alan sent over an update. It looks like the original website is backing off its claim that September is in a mental hospital. The hospital released a statement apologizing to all its patients for the HIPAA violation, reassuring that the employee who took the photo has been terminated and that further legal actions will be taken. The statement also denies they ever had a patient by the name of September registered there and asks the media out of concern for the privacy of their 112 other patients to please leave the area."

September sighed. "I almost wish the receptionist would've tried to hit you or something so you could've twisted her arm around her back. I haven't wanted to hit anybody in quite a while, but knowing she published Harmony's picture, I want to slap her."

"Just as well you didn't. It would have only confirmed her suspicions about you," said Melanie. "But I wish she would have resisted too."

Adam leaned against the doorjamb. "The question is how many people saw the article and copied the photo."

"And did Shyla see it. She will not dismiss the possibility that I'm here in Chicago." Harmony pulled on the blanket, shrouding her head. September grabbed it before Harmony pulled it off her shoulder. She blushed as she looked down at her baby.

Adam stepped back into the hallway. "If you don't need me, I think I'll go check on dinner now."

"Thanks, Adam, I need to get rid of my makeup and this uniform. I'll be right back, September." Melanie followed Adam downstairs on her way to the master bedroom. She stopped him in the hall, signaling for him to go into the formal living room. She sat on the couch and waited until Adam sat too.

"I try to stay out of my children's romantic lives, but you need to decide. Are you going to be a long-term part of September's and Harmony's lives, or is this temporary? Long-term it will be better for September to deal with the relationship status now. If you are not planning on making it permanent, you need to leave. If marriage is your plan, tell her. I'm not saying you need to propose this week, but if that is the general idea, give her time to start processing that you love her. Besides the PPD messing with her feelings, love has been in short supply in her life. Trusting yours will take time."

"Are you wanting an answer now? Or do you want me to think about it?"

Melanie crossed her arms and gave him one of those knowing mother looks. "I'm not the one who needs the answer." She walked into her bedroom and closed the door.

The smell of the shepherd's pie filled the kitchen, Adam's mouth reacting like Pavlov's dogs to a dinner bell. Roast beef and potatoes at their leftover best. Adam put on an oven mitt before checking to see if dinner was finished cooking. The mashed potato top looked perfectly toasted, so Adam removed the dish and set it on the rack to cool before setting the table. He heard the garage door indicating his father was home. He set a fourth place at the little kitchen table. It was probably the most people who ate here since the twins had left for college. When the Hastings gathered for their bimonthly family Sunday dinners, they ate in the dining room as they had every night when he was growing up.

His father came through the kitchen door, followed by Alan. Jethro scanned the room, brows furrowed. "Where are your mother and September?"

"Bedroom and nursery." Adam pointed toward both. "Is something wrong?"

"I'm not sure. Shyla called me."

Adam nearly dropped the plate in his hand. "She heard about the picture?"

Alan answered him. "She heard from Sven."

"She called to warn us. He's already booked a flight from LA. She's flying out in the morning."

"Why did she contact you?"

"Your mother and I have long been listed as September's emergency contacts. Shyla didn't even ask me to confirm or deny we've been helping September."

"Does Sven know about us?"

Alan grabbed a fifth plate from the cupboard. "He definitely knows about you."

At the sound of the footsteps in the hallway, the three of them stopped talking.

September had never experienced stage fright until she walked into the kitchen and the three Hastings men stopped talking to stare at her. She shifted Harmony on her shoulder. "I couldn't get her to burp. I wondered—"

Adam came and took Harmony. Almost instantly, the baby released a loud burp. Jethro crossed the kitchen. "That is some trick you have. I wish I had known that one, thirty years ago." He opened his arms, and September stepped in for a hug.

"I've been worried about you, kiddo. I'm glad you will be staying with us for a couple weeks." Jethro ended the hug.

"Are you sure I am not an imposition?"

Jethro took Harmony from Adam. "Are you kidding? I love having this little one around. The best part is Adam gets to get up in the middle of the night." He used a lighter tone, addressing the baby more than her.

Melanie came into the kitchen and opened the fridge. "Alan, nice you can join us. Put the salad on the table, will you? Adam, go get the bouncy rocker thing so September can use both hands to eat. And, September, be a dear and add some napkins to the settings. My barbarians always forget them until after they've spilled."

In a matter of seconds, they were all gathered around the table, holding hands for prayer. September found herself between Melanie and Adam as Jethro prayed.

"Now that we are all sitting, Alan, why don't you fill me in on why you've joined us, as I doubt it is because I used leftover pot roast in tonight's dinner." Melanie passed the food around the table as she spoke. September admired the way Melanie took control of the situation and moved it forward.

Alan scooped some of the pie onto his plate. "We were discussing a call Dad received." He looked from his father to September and back before continuing. "Shyla is coming out in the morning. She assumes we are helping September, but she didn't ask. She wanted to warn us that Sven is on his way too."

September's fork slipped from her fingers and bounced on the table before falling to the floor. She pushed back from the table. Where could she hide? Canada wasn't far. Adam put his hand on her knee. "Don't get up." He bent and retrieved her fork. "I'll get you another."

"I'm catching up on this case, and I need you to fill me in on some of the details. We need to figure out how much Sven knows about us and Adam." Jethro gave her almost the same look her father used to.

She took a deep breath before answering. "I'm not sure. He knows how I felt about Adam and that I've known the family forever. But pretty much anyone who knows me knows that. I don't think I talked much about anyone other than Adam." *Constantly, for months*. "If Shyla suspects you are helping me, it is likely he does too. Should I go to my house? No one but Melanie knows where it is."

Melanie shook her head. "I don't think there is a need to leave yet. Sven is more likely to show up at the office than he is here, as he would have to find the house. Shyla may show up here, but that is easily remedied. We will put a bassinet in the safe room, and you can be in there before she even rings the bell and we'll only keep baby paraphernalia upstairs. I'll keep one of the boxes Abbie brought over down here. I can always say I am expecting triplet grandchildren and I've started collecting for them."

"That's sure true," muttered Alan.

Melanie scowled at her second son. "We could have some of the female guards rotate through too. Visiting friends, housekeeper to help me in my old age, that sort of thing."

"I'll be here." Adam added a second helping of shepherd's pie to his plate.

Jethro forcefully set down his water glass. "You can't be. If Sven comes to the office, he will expect to find you. He'll follow you, and you need to lead him on the most boring day of his life. I think we need to do some surprise inspections of the buildings we monitor. Also, work on training Elle. He might assume there is an interest there."

"I don't like ZoElle involved." Alan crossed his arms.

"She needs the training on dealing with tails, etc., if she is going to work with us as a bodyguard," said Adam.

"But she isn't ready."

"Alan, this isn't your call to make. It's mine, and I think she is. She isn't your client anymore." Jethro sat back in his chair, his now-empty plate in front of him. September glanced at her own full plate. How could they eat at a time like this?

"So can I still come here at night?" asked Adam.

"Let's play that by ear." Melanie took some more salad. "If he thinks of attempting a paternity suit, he will need to wait until Tuesday when the courthouse opens again."

"Why would he want to do a paternity suit? He didn't want a baby." September covered her abdomen, memories of how much he didn't want a baby flooding her mind.

Adam grunted. "Control. Make your life miserable."

"I thought you didn't know him." September trembled.

"I read the file Alan put together on him. I know the type."

Melanie gathered the empty plates. "Why don't you take September and show her the safe-room access."

Adam leaned over. "Take two bites, then we will go."

She expected the food to taste like sand as her mouth was already dry, but the meat was tender, with a hint of hickory, and two bites weren't enough. Adam played with Harmony while she finished eating.

ADAM SQUEEZED SEPTEMBER'S HAND. "MOM, will you watch Harmony?"

"Sure, put a few baby supplies in the room along with the bassinet." Melanie bent over the bouncy seat.

September looked back over her shoulder, eyes wide.

He squeezed her hand again. "Don't worry. Mom will take care of her. I'm curious. You've been in this house several times over the years. Any idea where our hidden room could be?"

"No, I assumed those were things in old castles and mega-paranoid superstars' houses. Not a family of security guards." She paused at the entrance to the living room. "Behind the bookcase?"

"No. Dad designed it himself. Mom gave him the idea for the door." Adam opened the door to the linen closet next to his parents' bedroom and lifted the third shelf from the top. "You lift on the shelf and then push on the right side of the wall." The entire shelf unit slid into the wall, revealing a passageway. As Adam stepped across the threshold, low-wattage lighting blinked on to illuminate a windowless room.

September followed, brushing her fingers over the wall forming the side of the closet, past an open steel door and into a small windowless room. She gazed around the room, eyes wide. "I never would've guessed. I always thought a secret room should be behind bookcases or stairways, not the stash of towels."

"Mom's idea. No one would think to look behind the guest linens and spare rolls of TP." He led her over to a small screen the size of a tablet embedded in the wall. "From here you can watch all the camera feeds, including the one situated above the door to this room. There's food and water as well as a cell phone kept charged at all times and a dedicated landline with a number known only to members of the family." Adam pointed around the room to the various items. "This couch makes into a bed, and these two large panels will pull out into sets of bunk beds. We can put the bassinet in this corner. I don't see a scenario where you would be in here more than a half hour. The room is soundproofed, but it's best if Harmony doesn't cry for long." September wandered around the room, picking up books and a deck of cards. "Have you ever had to use it for long?"

"No, we've only used it for drills. Once we stayed in here for thirty-six hours during Christmas break. I was a teenager. It may have been around Y2K. Dad wanted to test the room in case of the worst. I remember Dad wanted two full days, but we discovered the mini porta potty could not accommodate seven Hastings for long."

She walked back over to the entrance. "How do I close the door?"

Adam stood close behind her. She'd used a different shampoo than last year, perhaps one the hospital provided. He reached around her and put his fingers into an indention on the back side of the closet where the sliding portion stuck out from the wall two inches. "Put your fingers here and pull. The rolling shelves slide easily. It automatically closes the closet door in the hallway. Try it." He removed his hand.

September placed her fingers in the groove and pulled. The closet slid easily on the tracks and closed quietly.

Adam took another step back beyond the frame of the security door. "Then you need to shut this door." Adam swung the heavy metal door in place and turned the huge vault-like dial until he heard the dead bolts engage. Then he opened the door. "You try. The vault door takes more pressure than a regular one."

September used both arms to crank the lock shut, then smiled up at him. He brushed a lock of hair off her brow and trailed his fingers down the side of her face the same way he had that fateful night. Every muscle in his body ached to reenact the kiss. She didn't move as he lowered his head. He wasn't sure if she was ready and tried to think of a way to ask without breaking the spell, but when she rested her hand on the center of his chest and rose on tiptoe to meet him, Adam closed the gap. Their lips met, tentative and questioning at first, but then the spark they'd ignited so long ago flickered brightly. No longer questioning, he pulled her closer and ended the kiss with an exclamation mark. He lifted his head but didn't step away, and September rested her head on his shoulder.

As they stood in silence, his mind raced faster than his heart, leaping ahead to the possibility of forever.

September stepped back first, a slight frown wrinkling her brow. "We need to go get the bassinet." She opened the vault and closet doors. As he exited the room, he heard her footfalls on the stairs. She hadn't run far, but still, she had run.

As soon as the lock clicked, September leaned back against the bathroom door and slid to the floor. Why had she kissed Adam? Dr. Brooks had warned her about making big decisions during the first few weeks of postpartum recovery. But then, loving Adam wasn't a decision, at least not a new one. She wasn't sure when her heart had chosen him. Most of the PPD mothers had a significant other. Was it so wrong for her to want Adam?

She used a deep-breathing technique to calm her heart. Kissing him felt so right. The hole in her soul wasn't merely being filled, it was being healed. But this was crazy. She was crazy. No, not crazy, she told herself again. Postpartum depression wasn't crazy. If she'd learned anything this week, she'd learned that. If there weren't so many other issues going on, she would have kissed him again and again.

Someone tapped on the door, and Melanie's voice floated through. "September, are you in there?"

September pushed off the floor. She shouldn't hide. The last thing she wanted was for someone to think the PPD had gotten worse. She opened the door to find Melanie standing in the hallway, Harmony asleep in her arms.

"I'm going to put her down. Come help me." September sensed there was more to the invitation than putting her daughter in a crib.

"Let's grab a few things for the safe room," whispered Melanie as they gathered diapers, a couple changes of clothing, blankets, and a box of baby wipes.

September followed Melanie out into the hall and down the stairs. No one else was in the safe room, but the bassinet now sat in the corner. Melanie arranged the baby supplies on a shelf. "Do you feel comfortable getting anything in and out of here?"

"I would like to practice. I'm afraid I might freeze up."

"There is a teddy bear in the boxes Abbie brought. Jethro can play with Harmony, and we can run a few scenarios." Melanie got the bear and her husband. After two practice rounds where September dropped the bear, Jethro decided on keeping the linen closet door open, as it couldn't be viewed from the entryway anyhow. September could then run in, place Harmony in the bassinet, and lock the door.

September unlocked the door again. "Is there a way you could get in here if I was in here and you aren't?"

"Yes, I can open the closet, and there is a keypad on the vault door requiring both a retinal scan and my fingerprint, as well as the code. Are you afraid of cramped spaces?" Melanie straightened the pillows on the couch.

September looked around the eight-by-ten room. It wasn't that small. Although her walk-in-closet in LA was larger. "Surprisingly, it doesn't seem cramped."

"Maybe I think the room is claustrophobic because I spent a day and a half in here with my husband and five children. Never let anybody tell you teenage boys can smell pleasant under such circumstances. I believe Abbie started wearing perfume shortly after our camp in. For months I carried a handkerchief in my pocket doused in perfume. I also added air fresheners to the stash of survival items in here."

"I can imagine. And with seven people in a room this size, it would feel confining." September put the bear in the corner of the couch, thinking Harmony might like the music it played.

Melanie checked the food cupboard. "With any luck, we will not need to use the safe room, but don't worry—even if Harmony screams, I doubt anyone will hear it. Jethro tested the soundproofing by putting all five children in here and asked them to scream. In retrospect, it wasn't such a good idea because Alan and Andrew decided they wanted to make sure Abbie screamed the loudest. Which started a fight with Alex, of course."

"You mentioned you suffered PPD after the twins were born. After you got help, how were you able to tell whether you were in your right mind or not?"

Melanie sat on the couch and patted the cushion for September to join her. "I'll admit there are times throughout my life I've wondered if I've ever been in my right mind. It's part of being a woman, part of being a mother, and maybe part of being human. PPD magnifies everything. Mole hills of laundry become mount wash-a-ton and keep growing. Chocolate either tastes like plastic or you devour it by the truckload, searching for the sweet kick it used to give you. The emotions you feel are either too intense or nonexistent. As you come back to yourself, you question everything. Part of it is recognizing your feelings. Remember the other night before you went into the hospital how you knew that what you were doing wasn't right?"

September shuttered. It wasn't something she wanted to feel again. She nodded.

"For me, part of knowing if I'm in my right mind is how the opposite feels. Not like trying to decide if I should wear the red dress or a green dress and not being able to come up with an answer. More like remembering I like sunshine and choosing not to go sunbathe in the snow because something feels wrong with that picture."

September pondered for a moment. "How do you know if something you're feeling is right or if the feeling's lying to you?"

"What were you thinking when you locked yourself in the bathroom?"

The change in direction startled September. "That I needed a minute to clear my head?"

"Why?"

"Because I wasn't sure if I should have kissed Adam."

"I'll assume this is a more recent development than last year. Don't answer. But in my experience, remembering back when the dinosaurs roamed the earth and I had my first kiss with Jethro, I had a lot of questions. I think it's natural to ask questions. In your case, you have a few more complications than the average kiss. May I ask if you came to any conclusions?"

"Mostly what-ifs. If I was in this same situation without Harmony, or PPD, or Sven as a potential threat, would we even be kissing?"

"I have an inkling based on what you've said about how you feel, or felt, about Adam over the past year. I'd say if your feelings now are along the same lines as they were three months ago, they are worth exploring," said Melanie.

Discussing her feelings with Adam's mom was weird, even if she'd first had the friendship with Melanie. Yet the words spilled out as if she were speaking to her own mother. "I think I still love him. I'm hoping it is not the antidepressants making me feel that way. There were several days this past month I detested him as strongly. I've wanted to lash out at him and blame him for everything. I know we talked about my choices and his choices, but sometimes I want him to hurt as badly as I do. The anger is almost uncontrollable. But I think the recent angry feelings are due to PPD. They aren't me. You know I was angry at him when you brought me back from Seattle, but this is different."

"I suggested in one of your family therapy sessions you discuss how it felt when he left you. Just because you are angry with him doesn't mean you don't love him."

"But I thought love wasn't supposed to feel so up and down."

"I think people think of love like a view of the mountains. From a distance they are gorgeous and serene, with their snowcapped peaks and evergreens, and you feel if you climb them you can go up forever. What most don't realize is when you walk through the mountains, there are valleys, curves, mudholes, and cliffs as well as breathtaking vistas. Love isn't a never-ending euphoria. It takes lots of work. Yes, I love Jethro more than I did almost forty years ago when we first met, but there have been times I wanted to push him off the next cliff and others when I wanted to wrap my arms around him and enjoy the view." Melanie put her hand on September's knee. "It is natural to be upset with Adam. Even with the noblest of intentions, he still left. That hurt. But are you going to keep working on climbing to the peak or wallow in some gorge?"

"So, this isn't all PPD mess?" September wiped her eyes.

"I don't know if even Dr. Brooks could tell you. Before the PPD, there was this battle in you over your feelings for Adam. One thing I did learn is that if a thought or feeling wasn't out of character for you five months ago, it isn't now. It may only be the intensity that's out of proportion. You are the same person. You still love candied pecans. I see no reason why you still can't feel the same for Adam." Melanie opened her arms.

"Thanks." September leaned in and gave Melanie a hug.

When the embrace ended, Melanie stood. "Let's go see where our men went."

THE NURSERY DOOR STOOD AJAR. Adam watched September rock Harmony to sleep. He tapped on the door. September looked up, a smile on her face. "She doesn't want to go to sleep."

"Would you like me to try?" He reached for the baby and settled Harmony on his shoulder. "Now, little one, Mama wants you to go to sleep." In response to being patted on the back, Harmony let out a large burp.

"Perhaps that's the problem. I can never get her to burp as well as you."

"It's only fair I have one talent in caring for babies." Adam sat on the ottoman, continuing to rub Harmony's back. "I'm wondering if I owe you an apology."

"For the kiss?"

"Not exactly. I'm not sorry I kissed you, but maybe for the timing?"

September bit her lip and continued to rock back and forth in the chair. "Timing is, well, everything. Perhaps, though, there isn't really a good time or a bad time to express our feelings. It's what we do after the expression. Do you feel differently than you did a year ago?"

Adam adjusted his hold on Harmony, who now dozed in his arms. Afraid of breaking the openness between them if they moved out of the bedroom, he kept his voice low as to not disturb Harmony's slumber. "If you mean am I still in love with you, the answer is yes. If you mean do I still feel our age gap or my being your bodyguard is a hindrance to our relationship, then no. I've had time to think over this past year, and I feel like it would've been better if I'd had somebody else take over as your head of security. I think I let the ten-year age gap play too big of a role. I was afraid it would put us on unequal footing. It wasn't until I worked other jobs that I realized you're emotionally older than most women your age." He paused. "*Older* is not the right word. Perhaps more mature. More experienced. I'm not saying this well."

September gave him a half smile. "I was emancipated at fifteen, making me an adult a good three years before anybody else my age."

"Like I said the other night, I'd like to try. I think someday we would make an awesome family, but I don't want to pressure you into any decisions, especially right now."

"At the dinner tonight, I feared somebody might suggest we get married immediately to protect Harmony and me."

"The thought crossed my mind." Adam shook his head. "But I wouldn't want you wondering if I married you to protect you."

"I hadn't thought of that. I was more worried about trying to decide when I'm not quite sure I'm all here." She tapped her head.

If he hadn't been holding Harmony, he would have pulled September into an embrace. "The very fact that you are questioning whether you are not all here probably means you are. However, I also want to respect Dr. Brooks' counsel that you don't make any major life-changing decisions in the next few weeks. Which is why I kind of feel I need to apologize for kissing you. I'm afraid it's pushing you into something you might not be ready for."

"Like I told your mom, or, rather, she pointed out, the kiss wasn't really a new choice or decision." She paused a moment.

Adam wondered what she was editing out. "With the thought of Sven and Shyla coming and with me having to figure out how to open the closet door while carrying a baby, it's been an emotionally full night. And that on top of the whole paparazzi thing. It seems like this day has lasted a hundred years."

Harmony's breathing shifted to the deeper breathing of a sound sleep. "Would it help if we do something a little normal? I can put Harmony down, and we could go curl up on the couch and watch a movie."

September closed her eyes and continued to rock back and forth. Then she nodded. "I think I would like that very much."

Adam knew he would too.

Somewhere, a baby was crying. September's pillow was so warm and the fading dream so happy she tried to hold on to both for one more moment, but the crying grew louder. She tried to sit up, but a weight held her down. Adam's arm was wrapped around her waist. Her pillow turned out to be his chest. She moved his arm and sat up as Melanie walked into the family room carrying a fussy Harmony.

"Oh, my, I didn't mean to fall asleep watching the movie. I don't even think we had a baby monitor down here."

Melanie handed September the baby. "I don't think she cried long. I already changed her diaper."

Adam stretched and yawned. "Sorry, Mom."

Melanie smiled before she waved and turned back toward her own bedroom.

"I should take her upstairs and feed her."

"You can feed her down here."

The gas fireplace made this room warmer than the ones upstairs. "You sure you don't mind?"

Adam shook his head and scooted to one side of the couch, and September sat down. She would not dare had Melanie not brought a blanket with Harmony. She fumbled with her nursing bra under her shirt. Fortunately, Harmony had her part down, and September started the feeding without any embarrassment. She leaned into Adam's side, and he put his arm around her shoulder. Perhaps this is what it would've been like if different choices had been made last year. Neither of them spoke, the only sounds in the room the fireplace and Harmony's eating. When she finished, Adam burped her, then balanced her on one shoulder and extended a hand toward September. "Let's get this little angel back to bed."

September took his hand. After they put the baby down, Adam walked September to her room. He cupped her hands in his. "When you wake up in the morning, I'll be gone. Deidre's team picked up Sven at O'Hare and followed him to his hotel. I need to get back to my apartment to start our game of cat and mouse. I'll be back Sunday afternoon for family dinner." When he didn't make a move toward her, September went up on tiptoe and pressed a kiss to his lips. Pulling her closer, he kissed her back. She slipped her hands out of his and wrapped them around his neck to hold herself firmly in place.

When she ended the kiss, he rested his forehead on hers. "I'll miss you." He stepped back and opened the door to her room.

September smiled to cover the ache in her heart. "Good night, Adam." She slipped inside the room and closed the door.

Sleep did not come as easily as it had in the family room with Adam. Whenever she closed her eyes, Sven's face loomed in the shadows. Try as she might, her mind insisted on replaying some of the worst moments of her life. She hugged her pillow, hoping the position would bring back memories of waking in Adam's arms.

After counting backward from twenty several times, September gave up and pulled out her journal.

I'm scared. What will Sven do? Who will he hurt? And it will all be my fault. I wanted to be held. I didn't realize what he was, or I didn't want to. Adam wants to work on our relationship. It is so complicated. That sounds cliché, but it is so true. I can't believe I fell asleep in Adam's arms tonight. Everything I've been searching for is there. He feels like home. I wish I had realized before that I wasn't going to find a sense of peace and security in just any bodyguard's arms. I wouldn't—Dr. Brooks says I shouldn't think like that. Adam thinks we have a second chance. I want it, but I need to be careful. I don't think this a mistake, but it is hard not to see things that way. Yet when I see Adam hold Harmony and cuddle her, I can't help but wish she was his from the very start.

The journal lay open on the floor, an ink scribble across the page. September squinted to read the clock. Not quite six. She checked the video monitor to find Harmony still asleep. Hoping Adam hadn't left yet, she dressed in an old pair of jeans, satisfied they mostly fit, and a nursing top. She took the monitor with her as she left the room.

Jethro and Melanie were in the kitchen eating oatmeal. "Morning, is Adam still here?"

"I think he left shortly after I brought Harmony down in the middle of the night," said Melanie.

"Oh." September grabbed a cup and poured a glass of milk. Until a few months ago she hadn't been much of a milk drinker despite the milk mustache ads she'd posed for a few years ago.

Melanie stood. "Sit down, and I'll get you some oatmeal. Hopefully, you can finish before—"

Sounds of Harmony filled the room.

Jethro pushed back from the table. "My turn."

"Are you sure?" September turned to leave.

"Hey, I'm almost a grandpa, and I need to practice. Abbie's triplets will be here before we blink twice."

September sat down and ate. She and Melanie eavesdropped through the monitor as Jethro changed Harmony and sang off tune.

Melanie turned down the volume. "He never could carry a tune, but he loves to sing. My poor grandchildren."

"I think he is ready to be a grandpa." September finished the oatmeal. "Thanks, it has been forever since I had it with maple syrup. I asked room service for maple syrup once, and they brought me the fake stuff. I've stayed with brown sugar ever since."

Jethro brought Harmony into the kitchen. "I don't think she likes my singing much. You spoiled her."

"I haven't sung much to her." September had sung little in the last few months. Her manager would be furious to learn she hadn't practiced in so long. She wasn't sure when she'd stopped singing. Until today, she hadn't even missed it.

Harmony let out a squawk, which translated to "Feed me now, or I'll start crying loud."

September took Harmony. "I'll go feed her, and you can get to work."

Jethro sat back down at the table. "It's Saturday and a three-day weekend. I get to stay here until Tuesday."

"I hope you are not staying on account of me."

"I already had the weekend off, which makes it very convenient to hang around here."

"And Adam?"

"He gets office duty this weekend. We decided we wanted to make him easy for Sven to find, which makes you harder to find."

Harmony fussed louder.

"If you will excuse me."

September sat in the chair in the living room. The walls were decorated with family photos. September studied them as Harmony ate. *What would Adam's children look like*? A dangerous thought to follow. September focused her thoughts on the lyrics of her favorite songs instead. Maybe it was time she start singing again.

Adam didn't have to wait long for the games to begin. Deidre called him a few minutes after he arrived at the office. "The tail I put on Sven says he ordered an Uber and drove to Eastland hospital. He paid the driver to wait, and looks like he is headed to the office now. I am working on swapping the Uber driver with one of my crew. I'm coming into the office now."

"Good, I need you at the front desk."

"What about Elle? I thought she wanted overtime."

"Alan put her on dispatch. Doesn't think she is ready for whatever may happen."

Deidre harrumphed. "I'll be there. Just because I am a woman, I'll man the desk."

"It has nothing to do with your gender. Its Saturday, and there are only four people here. I can't sit at the desk. Ditto for the dispatcher who is training Elle. Alan is in the monitoring room, and I'd rather Sven does not meet all the Hastings in one day." Adam once thought his sister had a chip on her shoulder about the female bodyguard thing, but compared to Deidre ...He shook his head. Not everything it the world was gender-based or biased, as the case may be.

"Sorry. I shouldn't assume."

Adam rubbed his temple. "I'll see you in a few."

Deidre arrived sooner than expected. "Everything's ready to make the driver switch when Sven gets here. He walked in and out of the hospital within three minutes. I don't think he learned anything."

"Probably not. You can't ask for a patient by name, and you need their code and to be on the approved visitor list. I don't think bluffing works."

"Do you have any idea how this will play out?" Deidre ran a hand over her dark hair and smoothed her jacket.

Adam straightened his tie. "No idea. Buzz me and I'll meet him out here and then move our chat into the small meeting room." Adam pointed to the glass-walled conference room at the side of the lobby. I don't want him getting a look at the back offices if I can help it."

Deidre's phone beeped. She tapped her earpiece. "Two blocks away."

Adam returned to his office and waited for Deidre to page him. He pulled up the front-desk camera and watched as Sven sauntered into the office and leaned on the reception desk.

Deidre smiled sweetly at him. "May I help you?"

"I'm here to see Mr. Hastings."

"And you are?"

"Sven Bent, from California."

"I'm sorry, Mr. Hastings is out today. Would you like to make an appointment? He has an opening Wednesday morning."

"I don't have until Wednesday morning to stay around waiting for your boss."

"I might be able to schedule something with Jethro Hastings on Tuesday." She was pushing his buttons, and the tanned and bleached-haired bodyguard was falling for it.

"Who is Jethro Hastings? I'm here to see Adam Hastings."

"Do you have an appointment?" Deidre played the secretary part well.

"No, I do not have an appointment. May I see Mr. Ȧdam Hastings?"

"I can see if he is available."

Sven leaned farther over the reception desk. "Do that." Sven muttered something else the audio didn't pick up. Knowing Deidre could take the man down almost as fast as Abbie used to, Adam admired her self-control.

"I'll ring him right now."

Adam picked up his phone and played along. "Yes?"

"Mr. Adam, there is a Sven ... what was your last name?" She covered the phone.

"Bent."

"Sven Bent here to see you. He doesn't have an appointment. Do you have a few minutes?"

"I'll be right out." Adam hung up the phone.

Sven continued to lean on the reception desk, tossing out pickup lines like peanuts at a zoo. Deidre batted her eyes, her usual demeanor hiding more of an actress than Adam suspected. He made a mental note to talk to Jethro about expanding Deidre's responsibilities. "I'd love to show you the city, but I'm already booked this weekend."

Adam suppressed a chuckle. The only thing Deidre would show him was how well she could put her fist through his mouth. He extended his hand to the man. "Mr. Bent, nice to meet you. How can I help you?"

Sven refused the offered hand. "Is there someplace we can talk?"

"Will this conference room work?" Adam gestured to the conference room, then turned to Deidre. "Hold my calls, will you?"

If Deidre could use her glare as a weapon, she would have no need for a gun. "Of course, Mr. Adam."

He closed the door behind them. "Now, Mr. —"

"Where is she?"

Adam half turned back to the lobby.

"Not the bimbo secretary. September Platt." Sven bit each word out.

"I don't know." *She could be in the kitchen or the living room.*

"She came here to have my baby, and I want that baby!"

"Congratulations on being a father. But I still can't help you."

Sven leaned across the table, hands fisted. "I know you know where she is. The trollop never stopped talking about you. Who else would she run to? There were no other men in her life, and her control freak of a manager has no idea where she is."

"We parted ways over a year ago. I am no longer in her employ."

Sven barked out a harsh laugh. "I know. I heard about your leaving her every day. Took me forever to get her to tumble in the sack with me. I'll tell you, it wasn't worth it. I guess you knew what you were doing when you didn't waste any time on her."

Adam schooled his reaction. Punching the jerk in the face wouldn't be prudent—yet. "Sorry, but I can't help you."

Adam walked out of the conference room.

"Can't, or won't?" Sven followed him into the lobby. "You give that little tart a message for me. She wasn't supposed to have the baby, and I'll make sure she will not keep it."

Adam crossed his arms to keep from leveling Sven. "Supposing I know where she is, do you think threatening her and her baby in front of the vice president of Hastings security will help your cause?"

Sven stepped closer. His breath stunk of onion bagel. He poked Adam in the chest. "You listen to me. She is mine. That baby is mine. No half-baked security team in Chicago will keep her from me. She owes me, and she needs to pay me for providing her with a child."

Sven pushed out the front door and into the elevator.

Adam locked the front door and turned to Deidre. "Good job with the receptionist gig."

"The jerk thought I would go out with him because he flexed his muscles. I have another idea of how I would like to take him out."

Adam smiled. "I'd like to see that. It would probably top the time my sister told a bodyguard off. He didn't see it coming when she flattened him."

"I've seen the video of her brilliant move. He had to weigh what she did twice. I asked her to teach me the move a few months ago. I think I have it down. Can't wait to use it." Deidre pushed the chair under the desk and stood. "We got the Uber driver switched out and should know where he is the rest of the day."

Adam headed to the tech room. "Come on back. Let's go over the footage with Alan. The guy's not too bright. Threatened me and September as well as Harmony."

Hearing the garage door slam, September stopped folding clothes. Melanie came in and set a bag and a large manila envelope on the table. "Your house is secure. Deidre's team switched over the monitoring system."

"Thanks for grabbing me more clothes." September folded the little pink jumper Harmony wore earlier in the week. Already it was too small. She couldn't believe how fast time went. She bit her lip before asking, "Has anybody heard from Sven or Shyla?"

"Sven visited the office earlier today. The meeting went as well as we expected. He attempted to bully Adam." Melanie smiled.

"Any chance they got the conversation on video?"

"I'm sure they did. But I also don't think Adam will show you the video."

Once the protector, always the protector. "Probably not."

"I spoke with Deidre. They put a tail on Sven, and he doesn't seem to have much of a plan. He did give up the Uber for a rental car. He keeps getting lost."

"Sven isn't much of a planner. At least not the way Adam is, where he sees all the possibilities up front and plans for them. Sven always has one plan, and if it doesn't go his way—" There was no point in expounding. She didn't want Melanie to know how bad things could get if Sven's plans didn't go the way he expected. "I've been trying to not think about him. It makes me mad that I ever even thought he could be anything like Adam."

Melanie wrapped her arms around September's shoulders, and September turned into the embrace. "At some point, you will need to forgive yourself. We all make mistakes, choices we wished we hadn't. We clean them up the best we can and move on. I don't look at Harmony and see the mistake. I see a little bundle of joy."

"We keep talking about this, but I keep feeling so stupid over it. Especially now." September wiped a tear away. "Sven is threating Adam. Shyla is coming, and I will have to face her. She deserves to know the truth."

Melanie picked up a onesie and folded it. "Let's get this stuff put away."

September put the last item in the basket. When Melanie's phone rang, she held it up so September could see the caller. "Shyla." Melanie put her finger to her lips and answered on speaker.

"Hello, Shyla, did you have a nice flight?"

"Peachy. Whoever said Hades was hot never visited Chicago in February when Hades freezes over. It is ten times worse."

"I thought Jethro told you there was no need to come out here. We aren't known for our pleasant winter weather."

"Enough chitchat. Where is she?"

"Where is who?"

"My client."

Interesting Shyla wasn't using September's name. She must be in a public place.

"I'm not sure who you mean."

"Melanie Hastings, I am tired of your games. I give you full kudos for the escape in the Seattle airport. The handing out of Cubs hats with a twenty-dollar bill to wear them was absolutely brilliant. How much did you spend on that little stunt?"

September covered her mouth. Melanie's ploy must have worked as planned. She'd hired a couple of locals from a temp agency to hand out dozens of Cubs hats along with a twenty-dollar tip for a "publicity stunt" on the concourse. Since September had gone into the bathroom with a Cubs hat on, to the guard watching her, the hat had to be the easiest part of her to spot. Who would watch for a gray-haired old lady in a red flowered muumuu and her pregnant friend returning from a trip to the islands?

"Shyla, by now you should know I don't do stunts. I protect my clients."

In the background, a car door slammed, and the change in audio carried the hollow sounds of a car system. "Whatever. If you don't have her, I have been working overtime to generate a story to keep her safe and out of Sven's way for nothing. She is better off with you. I don't think September could have lived with herself if she'd ended the pregnancy. I wanted to give her a chance to start over and hoped she would go running to you. I hadn't realized what I had done until it was too late."

"Wh—" September covered her mouth.

Melanie shook her head. "I think I am lost here."

"Surely he told her. I paid Sven to help her forget Adam."

Suddenly the room was spinning. September felt the world speed by, then nothing.

ADAM MADE A THIRD TURN. The same make and model Sven rented earlier that day now followed him. He headed for Abbie's gated mansion, then thought better. No point in getting his sister involved. The marquee for a gym in the chain he belonged to beckoned people to come in and work on their New Year's resolutions. Adam pulled into the lot. Sven could either freeze his California tan off or come in and get the free tour. In the meantime, Adam could work out some of his frustrations. September needed him, and he was stuck trying to bore Sven into another scheme.

His mother's report of Shyla's part in September's relationship was not entirely unexpected. Anything to keep September smiling and on stage, even if it cost her soul. But even he didn't think Shyla could stoop so low as to pay Sven to seduce September. Adam assumed she had only encouraged the relationship. Shyla swore she had been explicit in the instructions for kissing only. According to his father, Mom had been in rare form continuing the phone conversation. Promising Shyla to find September first and protect her from Sven. At the same time, Mom cradled September in her faint. In the end, his mother had agreed to meet Shyla at a restaurant this evening.

Adam grabbed his duffel from the trunk and headed into the gym. When he came out of the locker room, Sven stood at the front desk talking with one of the trainers. Adam was heading over to one of the treadmills to warm up when his phone beeped.

"Are you as tired of this guy following you as I am?" Deidre's voice held a trace of humor.

"A bit."

"How about we have some fun with him? I'm thinking maybe you meet me for dinner and we make it look like—" She let the inference hang.

"Sounds like a good idea. Anyplace in mind?"

"Nothing too fancy, but not too cheap."

Adam looked up the restaurants in the area. "There's a Cheesecake Factory somewhere near. He'll have a difficult time following both of us if we leave from different exits."

"See you at seven thirty?"

"Me and my tail."

Adam waited until Sven was in the middle of his orientation before leaving the gym.

After seven miles on the treadmill in the Hastings' home gym, she should be exhausted, but the anger and frustration had her feeling like she could run forever. Melanie should be back from her meeting with Shyla anytime now. Jethro came into the room carrying Harmony. "I'm sorry to interrupt you, but this little one seems to think I am no longer adequate entertainment."

She switched the treadmill off. "Give me a minute to change?"

September returned in a flash. Harmony wailed. "Was Mom gone too long?" She took Harmony from Jethro and sat in her favorite chair.

Jethro followed a moment or two later, having given September time to situate Harmony. He opened a book. "I see you were working off some of your emotions this afternoon. It's a good way to do it. I've run a few marathons that way."

"You ran marathons?"

"I meant figuratively. When the boys were teenagers, I averaged ten to twelve miles a day plus an extra five for Abbie."

"I can't believe Shyla paid Sven to be my boyfriend and then I had to pay him to shut up about being my boyfriend."

Jethro slammed the book closed. "You paid him?"

September calmed Harmony. "He threatened to go to the tabloids and ruin my reputation. It was blackmail. I didn't know what else to do."

"Plus whatever your manager paid after you disappeared was enough to set him up in the LA area with his own firm. Any idea how much in total?"

September shrugged. "I paid him $300,000. No idea what Shyla paid. Sometimes I wish none of this ever happened. But when I'm holding her, I can't wish her away. How can something so stupid also be so good?"

"That is the kicker. Almost every time something terrible happens, something just as good happens to balance it out, if only we can find it."

"How do I find the good, there has to be more than just Harmony?"

"You do what the rest of us do. You keep on moving. Right now it's a difficult time for you. I remember when Melanie went through a similar rough patch after the twins were born. She had days where she did not think she would make it through. Add the complication of both Adam and Alan running around the house smearing peanut butter all over each other and the walls and anything else they could get a hold of. Melanie needed help to get by. ...we're here for you September."

"Thanks, Jethro. I know you are. I think that's why I came back here. Because I knew that despite what happened with Adam, you would still be here for me."

Jethro turned the book over in his hands. "I don't know if I should tell you this or not, but I believe Adam never stopped caring for you. But maybe you've figured that out by now."

September burped Harmony. The process became easier each time, but she still wished Adam were there as he did it so much more efficiently. "I am trying to work on my feelings. I guess the whole family is rooting for me and Adam."

"I think Andrew will be the happiest not having to deal with his surly older brother. If it's any consolation, Adam missed you. His grousing and his warnings about client relationships probably helped push Abbie into falling in love with Preston more than kept her away. You know how she always has to prove her brothers wrong."

"I can't wait to meet the man who got Abbie's heart." She laid Harmony in her lap and spoke to her.

"Preston and Abbie should be here for our regularly scheduled Sunday dinner. And it happens to be the twins' birthday. Having everyone here, we can have Adam over to the house with no suspicion from Shyla or Sven if he is following Adam. So you know, Adam and Deidre are having dinner tonight and trying to make things look like they are in a romantic relationship to see if they can get Sven to give up and go back home. He wanted me to tell you, so you didn't hear it another way and think the worst."

"Thanks for letting me know." *He wants me to trust him. Funny thing is, I trust him more than I trust myself.*

The door connecting the garage to the kitchen opened, and Melanie came in holding up a bag. "I brought leftovers." She set the bag in the kitchen and joined Jethro on the couch. "Shyla spent most of the time trying to figure out where I had you hidden. She assumes I know where you are and is acting on that assumption."

September picked up Harmony's giraffe and dangled it above the baby. "She pushed the relationship, and it probably had a lot to do with what happened. Still, I can't blame her for the choices I made. Though I can blame her for not looking out for me.

I decided before Harmony's birth I would not use Shyla as my manager anymore. Even if I have to let her contract run out. Adam used to tell me she controlled me much more than other managers did their singers. I guess because I was a minor, part of her never quite let me grow up. Do you think I should call her?"

Melanie shrugged. "I'm not sure. Let's see how the rest of this weekend goes. I got the impression she was using me as a messenger. She attempted to follow me, but I lost her on the tollway."

Harmony craned her head to look at the others in the room. Jethro pulled an afghan onto the floor and laid Harmony on it, singing a tune about markets and piggies.

Melanie covered her ears. "Honey, please stop. September, rescue us!"

A silly ditty about a little blue man her mother had sung when September was little came to mind.

"One morning when I was out shopping..." The notes came out clear, not rusty, as she expected. Harmony wiggled and batted her arms, and September sang another song.

During the second verse, Jethro's and Melanie's phones beeped at the same time.

The alarm.

Melanie scooped up the laundry basket and hurried down the hallway. September grabbed Harmony and followed. By the time she reached the safe room, Melanie had already set the laundry basket down inside. "Good luck. Watch on the monitor."

September set Harmony in the bassinet and locked the door. Startled by all the activity, Harmony began to whimper. September wanted to do the same. But she needed to be strong for her daughter, so she rocked Harmony, held her close, and sang her a lullaby.

TENSION WOUND ITS WAY AROUND the family dinner like spiderwebs encircling the room. After last night's false alarm, everybody was on edge. Even with all seven Hastings in the house and Preston and Abbie's bodyguards sitting outside, the anxiety didn't abate. Across the table, September laughed with Abbie over some joke about pregnancy Adam wasn't qualified to understand.

He had yet to speak with September alone. She looked well despite last night's scare. He watched Harmony in the bouncy seat as she batted at her mobile. Before long, her eyes drooped and closed.

Halfway through dessert, Jethro's phone beeped the alarm signal again. "Adam, go with her."

Adam scooped up Harmony and the seat and raced with September to the safe room. Once there, he set down the seat and locked the door.

"You are staying in here?"

"Dad told me to go with you. And since I wanted to, I'm glad to have his okay."

"But what if it is Sven? Your car is out front."

"Sven won't get past Preston and Abbie's bodyguards. As we left, Andrew put the extra dining room chair away and plans to tell whomever that I'm in the half bath off the mudroom with intestinal issues. He'll lock the door. Sit down."

September transferred Harmony to the bassinet first. "I am surprised she didn't wake up when I scooped her off the floor so fast."

"The lights-and-sound thing Abbie brought sure kept her entertained. Do you want me to turn on the monitor?" As much as he wanted to know what was going on, he didn't want to frighten September.

She bit her lip. "Keep the volume low. I didn't turn it on last night and wish I had. The wrong house for pizza delivery wasn't worth the panic I felt."

"How did you cope?" Adam turned on the monitor. Their visitor stood on the other side of Preston's guards where the camera didn't reach.

"I sang. It felt good. I haven't sung for weeks. Before the alarm sounded, Jethro was singing to Harmony, and your mom asked me to sing something better."

Adam watched the screen. His father joined his sister's bodyguards and was talking to someone. He assumed it wasn't Sven because the person stood shorter than the three men out there.

September hummed a few bars before launching into the chorus of one of her top-one-hundred hits.

I'm falling in love again with you, and even tho it's too good to be true—

I wonder if it could be, that you are falling in love with me ...

Not for the first time, Adam wondered if she had written a song for him. September sang only the first couple words of the second verse before she stopped and gasped, covering her mouth with her hand. She pointed at the monitor.

Adam turned to see what she was looking at.

"Do you mind if I turn up the volume?"

September shook her head and nodded, then shook it again. "I mean yes, turn up the volume, please."

Jethro offered Shyla a seat in the living room—the one where the camera had the best view.

Shyla didn't use any small talk. "I am not going to beat around the bush. I am sure you know where September is, and I'm also sure you are underestimating Sven. He called me an hour ago after being kicked out of the hospital again. He said he's calling his lawyer and is going to press kidnapping charges against Adam."

"Why?" asked his mother.

"He got someone to admit a baby had been abandoned at the office a week ago."

September grabbed Adam's arm. "I did not abandon Harmony. I placed her."

Adam pulled her into a half hug and then watched the screen, mesmerized.

Jethro turned in his seat, presumably to give Adam a better view. "I don't see how he can press kidnapping charges based on his theory."

"He's been to the police station a couple times; says he knows the police were investigating the presence of the child."

Melanie shook her head. "I still don't see how he can claim kidnapping when both of you seem to be ignorant to the gender. Illinois birth records are not public. Since Sven wasn't married to September at the time of birth, he isn't listed as the father."

"I knew you had been helping her."

"And what exactly is it you are doing?" Melanie crossed her arms.

Adam muted the volume for a moment. "Don't worry. Mom didn't reveal anything she didn't intend to."

September clung tighter to him. He rubbed her back, hoping she would feel the calm he didn't.

Shyla looked directly into the hidden camera in the living room. "I assume she's either on the other end of this video or you are recording it for her. Don't look so shocked. I've been in the business longer than most. I can spot most cameras a mile away. That one is very well hidden." She stood and came toward the camera. "September, I have a lot of things to apologize for. One of those things is not realizing how villainous Sven was when he came to work for me. I should never have tried to force you into an abortion. I wouldn't have let you go through with it. But I was reasonably sure the threat would send you running back to the Hastings, where you would be safest. There is a way to stop Sven. I think you know what it is as well as I do. Only you might not know I have evidence. I'm only going to talk to you one-on-one. This is not going to be recorded. When you are ready to talk, Melanie knows where to find me."

Shyla looked around the room. "Should I stay here or go wait for a call?"

Jethro shifted in his seat again. "We can try to reach out and contact her. It will be September's decision whether she talks." Jethro stood and showed Shyla to the door. "Now, we were in the middle of celebrating the twins' thirty-second birthday. Fortunately we didn't light the candles before you interrupted us. Please do not come back here again. Sven probably tailed you."

Adam waited until the front door closed behind Shyla before pulling September into a full hug. She buried her face in his chest. They stood together long after the all-clear signal beeped.

The urge to kiss her consumed him, but he knew the timing was wrong. "Why don't we take Harmony out and get some cake? We can figure out what to do after consuming chocolate."

September pulled back and gave him a half smile, then nodded before stepping out of his embrace and gathering her daughter in her arms.

Melanie placed two cakes on the table, one chocolate and one vanilla. Abbie gave Alex a mournful look. "Trade me cakes this year?"

Preston wrapped his arm around his wife's shoulders and looked at Alex. "Don't do it. Keep the chocolate for yourself."

Alex pulled the entire cake plate in front of him.

"But chocolate! I crave chocolate." Abbie reached for the cake. Preston held her back. He got an elbow in the ribs for his efforts—a playful jab, but even a pregnant Abbie could take down most men.

He spun his wife around and planted a huge kiss on her lips. "You wound me, lady."

Abbie looked into her husband's eyes. "If you are trying to get me to forget about chocolate, that didn't work." She turned back to Alex. "Please?"

Adam swiped the cake and cut a piece for Abbie.

September stifled a giggle. She forgot how much fun being around the Hastings could be. Harmony stirred, and September looked over to see her face redden. "Excuse me. Duty calls."

With so many men in the room, September took Harmony upstairs.

"Well, sweetheart, you missed all the fun. You slept right through it." September gathered a new diaper. "What are we going to do? I don't want her finding you. Charging Adam with kidnapping is crazy, but Sven is crazy. It will cause all sorts of problems. Don't worry, little one. Sven will never touch you. Adam will protect you if I can't."

Someone tapped on the door. September picked up Harmony and turned to see who it was. "Come in, Adam. The dirty deed is done."

"I only have a few minutes. We assume Sven followed Shyla. Once everyone starts leaving, I have to go too."

September nodded, not trusting herself to answer. Adam stepped closer and traced her cheek. "I don't want to leave you."

September leaned into his hand and nodded, knowing if she

spoke she would cry.

Adam wrapped his arms around both of them and kissed the top of September's head. "Both of you keep safe." He kissed Harmony's cheek, then September softly on the lips. She pressed for more, but he slipped out of the embrace and out of the room.

September sat in the rocker and hoped no one else would come in while she cried.

AS HE NEARED THE ON-RAMP, Adam debated between Wisconsin, Indiana, and rural Illinois. His father's plan was simple: send Sven on a goose chase as long as possible, giving September time to talk with her manager. He didn't like the plan, but then, he had never been much of a fan of Shyla. The woman could prove to be more dangerous than Sven as she knew how to manipulate September a hundred ways.

Deciding on rural Illinois, Adam headed west, out of town. After a half mile, he looked in the rearview mirror to see Sven tailing him. Knowing the bodyguard would expect evasive moves, Adam took detour after detour, careful not to lose Sven completely.

A light snow fell, though not enough to make road conditions hazardous, yet. Not wanting to travel farther from home and September, Adam pulled off the highway and into an all-night diner.

He requested a corner booth and ordered a cup of hot chocolate with whipped cream, then waited for Sven.

The California bodyguard didn't disappoint. He tromped across the diner and slid into the seat opposite Adam. "Having fun yet?"

Adam stirred his hot chocolate. "Depends on what you think of as fun. If you mean leading a bodyguard who is more brawn than brain halfway across the state for no reason other than my amusement, then I'm having fun. And you?"

"Why, you, I'll—" Sven started to rise from his seat.

Adam shook his head. "You're drawing attention. I don't know if you really want to spend time in jail in whatever town we happen to be in. Then again, maybe you enjoy comparing jails. You have been in a few, haven't you?"

Sven slid his menu to the end of the table. Behind him, a pair of Illinois Highway Patrol officers entered. Adam looked at his hot chocolate so as to not give anything away. When he'd chosen the diner, he hoped it was the type of establishment police would stop by in stormy weather.

In his anger, Sven had forgotten one of the cardinal rules of being a bodyguard—always use the lookout advantage. With his back to the door, he didn't see the interest the officers took in their escalating conversation.

"Tell me where she is!" Sven leaned across the table as far as he could without standing.

"In your dreams." Adam leaned back and took a sip of his hot chocolate, forcing himself to appear relaxed.

Slap!

Sven sent the cup flying, hot chocolate splattering across the bench and table.

"Hey!"Adam took the napkin already in his hand and wiped his face, then stood, keeping Sven's attention on him. Sven jumped up and took a swing, which Adam dodged.

"Tell me—!" He lunged for Adam, but the officers grabbed Sven before he could finish his sentence.

"Is there a problem here?" asked one.

Adam kept from smirking. "This man had the impression I am hiding an old friend from him. If I was, you can see why."

Sven struggled to release himself from the officers.

"Hey, cool down." The other officer looked over his shoulder to where a waitress stood motionless. "Call the locals, please." He pulled out a pair of handcuffs.

Sirens wailed in the parking lot. A pair of policemen came hurrying into the diner. The waiter pointed back to the corner where Adam stood with the officers. "Put this man on a drunk and disorderly. He is probably high. We'll help you get him in the car."

As the officers left the diner with Sven, Adam pulled two twenties from his pocket and set them on the table.

The manager rushed up. "You don't need to pay. Thanks for not hitting him back."

"No, problem. I had a feeling he was going to take a swing. Have a good evening, sir."

Adam returned to Chicago and his parents' house knowing that for at least the next few hours, Sven would be very busy. Or not. And he had a few more precious hours with September.

"You didn't bring your baby." Shyla looked around the meeting room at the Hastings Security office.

"No. I felt we could talk better without her." September had no intention of letting Shyla meet Harmony until they resolved things.

"I know you are not pleased with me. I assume you got the message I left at the Hastings' home."

"I understand you have proof that should keep Sven away from us. Although how, I have no clue. Eight months ago you told me not to go to the police because they wouldn't believe me despite my injures. Now you have proof?"

"How do you think I kept Sven from flapping his gums to any tabloid that would listen? Of course I have proof. I document everything."

Screaming would be a very appropriate reaction; however, it would bring everyone in the office to September's side. "So, if I had gone to the police—"

"The media would have known."

September nearly jumped out of her chair. "Who cares! He tried to kill Harmony! And he injured me bad enough we had to cancel the Dallas show. Do you know how much pain I was in? But I listened to you and trusted your advice. You want me to trust you now?" Out of the corner of her eye, she could see Jethro watching from the reception desk. September turned to the wall and took two deep breaths, searching for the triggers Dr. Brooks taught her in one session, and found none. Emotions were not the enemy, and the anger flowed through her justifiably.

After Sven left the hotel suite, September had laid on the floor for what seemed like hours before crawling to the hotel phone to call Shyla as the cell phone had been in her purse and was farther away. September turned to face her manager. "I think you should show me the evidence."

Shyla pulled out her tablet. "Before I show you this, I should say I'm sorry. I was wrong. We should have gone to the police, and I probably should have taken you to the hospital. I was more focused on your contracts and your reputation."

Adam had always warned her Shyla was looking out for herself more than she was September. She merely nodded at the apology, not ready to forgive yet not sure what to say.

Shyla swiped the screen and brought up the video. It took September a moment to place the video. The camera must have been above the television of her hotel suite in Dallas. The feed showed the night she invited Sven into the hotel room so she could tell him she was pregnant. It was the first time in three months she'd let him in. In the video, her hands shook as she wondered what his reaction would be and if he would marry her for the baby's sake. They sat on opposite ends of the couch. September always talked too much with her hands. The silent video triggered the replay in her mind of the exact words she had said.

"I know I've been putting you off. But I think maybe we should reexamine our relationship."

"Relationship? We didn't have much of that, but I'll be glad to take you back in that bedroom and show you what we did have."

The September on the video shook her head. "I'm pregnant."

Sven lunged toward her. "You're what?"

"I'm pregnant."

"Why, you little—you try to pin it on me?"

"Sven, you know you're the only one I've ever—"

Slap!

September watched as her head whipped back before Sven lunged at her again, this time his hands around her neck.

"Turn it off! Turn it off!" September covered her mouth with her hands to keep from screaming and bringing all the Hastings into the room. "How could you? How could you know the whole time that I was telling the truth and not do anything about it? I can't believe you were videotaping me! How often did you record me?"

Shyla put the tablet's cover over the screen. "For security reasons, I monitor almost every hotel room you're in and your dressing rooms. It's all in your contract."

"Did you video our kiss?" The private moment with Adam didn't need to be shared.

"No. I don't monitor your bedroom." Shyla had the nerve to look slightly disgusted.

"No, not what I did with Sven. I can't believe you knew and did nothing. My kiss with Adam was special. Please tell me it's not on video somewhere."

Her manager squirmed.

"It is, isn't it? Is there any part in my life that's been private?"

"I've shared nothing unless it was to protect you." Shyla lifted her chin and slipped the tablet back into her bag.

"What did you share?"

"I showed this video to Sven when I got him to sign a nondisclosure agreement and paid him enough money to start his own firm."

September didn't want to hear any more about what her manager had recorded or who had seen them. The fact that the recordings even existed was enough.

"The video should be enough evidence to go to the police and charge him with assault." Perhaps if she could focus on the main reason she'd agreed to meet with Shyla, it would help.

"I've asked a few discreet questions of a couple attorneys I know. I believe Sven can be charged on two counts of attempted murder. Since both of you signed contracts stating I could monitor you and the footage is legal, it will stand up in court. In the audio, he can be heard quite clearly yelling he will kill the baby as he repeatedly kicks you in the stomach."

It was all etched in her brain. How many nights had she woken up hearing the things he'd said and clutching her middle, trying to protect herself and her unborn child?

"I didn't play the audio for you because I figured it would be difficult to hear."

September wiped her eyes. "*Difficult to hear*? I hear it almost every night. He left me unconscious on the hotel room floor, probably assuming I was dead. At the very least hoping I would miscarry my child. And you knew!" September got up to leave. She needed Jethro and Melanie. And Adam, wherever he was.

"Wait! If you agree, we can turn this in and file charges. You're lucky it happened in Texas, where there's likely to be a conviction."

September shook her head in disbelief. "Lucky? How can you even say that?"

"Because other states only prosecute the assault on you. So you are lucky the attack happened in Dallas rather than on your next stop. And you're lucky I took photos of you the next day. Sven should be behind bars for quite a while. And the evidence is so damning most trial lawyers will talk Sven into cutting a deal, saving you from appearing in court. If you play your cards right, you can keep most of it out of the public eye. Show the media your darling child at the right time. Release a new song about second chances and starting over. Your fans will love it. Instead of being a fallen woman, you'll become a survivor."

"I won't *become* a survivor because I already am one. And as far as the rest, I don't care what my fans think about me. I lived this life for ten years. I'm enjoying not worrying every moment what everybody thinks about me. Yes, I keep looking over my shoulder to make sure I'm not recognized because my daughter is worth more to me than every stupid blogger in the universe who is going to write derogatory articles. I'll stand for her. I am already surviving."

"I see motherhood is changing you for the better." Shyla held out her hand with two thumb drives in it. "These drives contain identical copies of the video I showed you. The video goes until Sven leaves the hotel room. I've erased all other videos I have of you. It was one thing to keep track of you when you were fifteen; it's another now that you are twenty-five. I'm not sure when you grew up and I couldn't let go." She gathered her bag. "I'm thinking now might be a good time for me to retire. Make sure you send me a Christmas card." Shyla walked out of the conference room and out of the office.

September turned over the thumb drives in her hands, then ran into the arms of Melanie.

Adam! I need you.

HEAVY SNOW WAS FALLING BY the time Adam pulled into his parents' driveway around midnight. Only the security lights illuminated the house. The debriefing on what happened when September met with Shyla would wait till morning. Adam entered through the front door and re-enabled the house alarm. He took off his wet coat and shoes by the door. In the upstairs hallway, light seeped from the crack around the nursery door. He scratched lightly on it in case Harmony was asleep.

"Come in." September's voice drifted through the air like a lullaby. He pushed open the door to find September rocking a sleeping Harmony. "They say you're not supposed to let them fall asleep in your arms once they get to be this age, but I couldn't help it. She's the sweetest thing in the world."

She was wrong. The sweetest thing in the world was watching September rock her daughter.

Adam sat down on the ottoman opposite September. "I didn't believe in love at first sight until I met Harmony. I think she had me wrapped around that little fist of hers the first time she waved it at the office."

"It was the same for me when she was born. I never loved somebody as much in my entire life as the second they laid her in my arms. Those first couple weeks were magical, and then I hit a dark patch …"

Adam reached for September's free hand. "And you became one of the bravest women I know. It's never as easy asking for help, especially when the stakes are so high."

September rocked in silence for a few minutes. "Thank you for being the father she needed. You're a good man, Adam Hastings." She gave him a little smile, and even in the dim glow of the night light, he could tell she was blushing.

"What happened with Shyla?"

"She's been recording my whole life. Everything. She claims she threw all but one video away, but I don't know I trust that."

"Everything?"

"Everything. All our conversations. Friends. Anything that happened outside of my bedroom she reported. She claims she's destroyed everything she has."

"How did she do it? I checked the rooms for the last three years searching for cameras."

September shrugged. "The one video she didn't destroy was taken from somewhere around the TV in Dallas. It's of the night I told him I was pregnant."

"I assume that's the evidence she said she had?"

September nodded. "I still can't believe she knew everything and didn't help me. She only did what she thought was best for my career. You were right all along. I should have listened to you. But I guess with her listening to our conversations, she knew exactly what to say to keep leading me on."

Adam reached over, lifted Harmony from September's arms, and placed her in the crib. Harmony sighed in her sleep and snuggled into a new position on her back. Adam turned to September with outstretched arms. She stood from the rocker and walked into them. The tears in her eyes glistened, then fell as he gently walked them backward out of the room into the hallway so September's sobs wouldn't disturb Harmony's sleep.

"So what is on the video?"

September pushed back from him a little and looked him in the eye. "My nightmare in full color. Shyla thinks it's enough to get him tried for two counts of attempted murder in the state of Texas." She leaned back into him, and Adam wrapped his arms around her. Sven had beaten her. The man was lucky he was locked up in jail in some little town. "He tried to kill you?"

She nodded into his chest. "In Texas, you can try someone for attempting to kill an unborn child by harming the mother."

He wanted to see the video.

He didn't want to see the video.

"What are you going to do with it?"

She shrugged. "I am not sure. I am having a hard time dealing with it all. I'm so angry, and I don't know if I should be or if it is the PPD."

He rubbed her back. "I am angry too. It is a good thing Sven is locked up right now, and I'd much rather hold you than go after Shyla. And there is no way I have PPD."

She pulled back and gave him a half smile. "Thanks. It is hard for me to recognize which is which. It will probably be a few months before I dare trust my feelings."

"Be as angry as you want with Shyla and Sven."

She snuggled back into his arms. He placed a kiss the only place available, the top of her head, but September rose up on her toes and kissed him fully on the lips. "Adam Jedidiah Hastings, you are the best man I know."

He kissed her again, not sure what to say. He was so far from being the best man she knew. If he was, he wouldn't have run away from his feelings a year ago.

"We should probably get to bed so we can figure out the next steps in the morning." Either that or he would keep kissing her all night.

"How long will they keep him in jail?"

"Up to seventy-two hours. It depends on if the judge will be in on President's Day."

She nodded against his chest. "I am too tired to think."

He held her at arm's length. "Go get some sleep."

She turned to walk down the hall, then stopped. "Will you get Harmony during the night, please?"

Remembering what Dr. Brooks had said about the role of sleep deprivation in PPD, Adam agreed. "Do you want to feed her, or should I use a bottle?"

"A bottle. Thanks."

She turned into her bedroom, the click of the door echoing in the hallway and some place near his heart.

Something woke Adam. Harmony wasn't crying, but he went to check on her anyway. By the nightlight's glow, he could discern Harmony's sleeping form. He was just turning to go back to his own room when something caught his eye. A folded note sat on the rocking chair. Adam tiptoed across the room to retrieve it.

> *Adam,*
> *Please take care of Harmony. I'll be back as soon as I can.*
> *I love you,*
> *September*

THE EARLY-MORNING FLIGHT CATERED TO business people who needed to be in Dallas before eight. Due to the Monday holiday, it was only partially full. As the flight took off, a fear September never felt before gripped her. She closed her eyes and tried one of Dr. Brooks' meditation exercises. Statistically, a fear of flying was irrational. But she couldn't help it. Who would take care of Harmony if the unthinkable happened?

September concentrated on what she must do. Thinking about Harmony, she added another thing to her list—purchase a breast pump as soon as they landed.

September spent most of the flight writing out in code exactly what she would tell the Dallas police. If she came across as too weak or unbalanced, they might ignore her. Too unemotional would yield the same. Finally, those acting coaches might be worth what she paid them for since neither of the two movies she'd acted in were blockbusters.

For the billionth time, Adam checked his phone. September hadn't answered his texts or his voicemail.

"Stop pacing, son." Jethro put a hand on Adam's shoulder. "Trust her. Last week you thought she was on some irresponsible bender when she left Harmony at the office. How did that turn out?"

"She is the bravest person in the world. And although somewhat irrational from most people's perspective, she did the best thing she could do for her baby."

"She said she would be back, so trust her."

"But where could she have gone?"

"My guess is she went to Dallas."

"Dallas! A flight in this snow?"

"It stopped snowing at two thirty this morning. O'Hare has been running normally."

"Okay. I set the alarms. How did she get out?"

"I gave her the code."

Adam took a seat by the window and looked out at the snow resuming its onslaught. He should pray it ended so September could return as soon as she could.

Sounds of Harmony waking from her morning nap carried over the monitor.

Adam stood. "Sounds like I am on dad duty."

The Dallas Police Department lobby was lighter and cleaner than she expected. Perhaps she had watched too many New York City–based crime TV shows. She told the officer at the desk that she wished to report a crime. His eyes widened when she handed over her driver's license. An officer ushered her back to a private conference room where a female detective met her.

"I'm Detective Overton." The woman extended a hand in greeting. "Do you mind if I record our meeting?" The officer held up a digital recorder.

"That is fine." September took a seat and detailed the events that had unfolded in the Dallas hotel last summer. She handed over one of the flash drives. "This contains video of what I told you. I was unaware of its existence until yesterday. I had no idea my manager recorded me. I don't really want to watch it. But I will verify its contents."

"You haven't seen this?"

"I saw part of the video on my manager's tablet. She gave me the flash drive. But I haven't dared watch it all. I lived it once."

"Do you mind if I go get my laptop?"

"Sure." Right now she wanted the day to be over.

The detective stopped by the door. "Would you like anything? A bottled water, perhaps?"

"Yes, please."

The detective returned with a laptop and plugged in the thumb drive. The same video Shyla played yesterday started. Only this time the audio was on. September bit her lip at the first time Sven lunged for her.

Detective Overton paused the video. "If you would prefer, I can put on my headphones."

"I haven't been beyond this point, but I don't entirely trust my manager. I think this once I need to watch to make sure it isn't edited."

The detective turned the video back on, and they watched in silence, the video ending as Sven exited the hotel room and slammed the door.

"I will get this to the DA immediately. One more question. Why didn't you go to the hospital or report this crime last summer?"

"I made the mistake of listening to my manager. She said you wouldn't believe me and it would only bring unwanted attention. Since I could get up and walk the next day, she talked me out of going to the ER as well. The next afternoon, I managed to sneak a visit to a walk-in care center. I paid in cash and used a false name."

"Here in the Dallas area?"

September nodded.

"You used an assumed name?"

September opened her bag and pulled out an ID card with the name S. Rayne Platt. "Most places that don't require high scrutiny will take this, and legally, it is a variation of my name. I can give you the name of the doctor as well."

"If we can get you to sign a release for the results of the medical examination, it will be easiest. If you have time, I can have a pair of officers drive you over to the clinic and you can get a copy yourself. There's probably ample evidence in the video, but I'm sure the doctor listed your injuries. Let me guess, you told the doctor you fell down the stairs?"

September nodded. "She didn't believe me for a minute, especially with the bruising on my throat. She may have suspected who I really was. It wasn't like I could hide behind my sunglasses and floppy hat during the examination."

"I'm going to call the DA. I don't think I need anything else from you at this time. Do you know where Sven Bent is now?"

"He was arrested last night in a small west Illinois town. Sorry I don't know which one. I think he is still there."

"Are you planning on staying in Dallas?"

"Do I need to? I need to get back to my baby and booked a flight out of DFW at two thirty."

"As long as you've given me a valid way to contact you, there's no reason for you to stay in town. I'll have some officers take you over to the clinic, and then they can take you to the airport." Detective Overton cleaned up her notes.

"I'll take the ride to the clinic, but I'd rather not garner any extra attention by showing up at the airport in a police car."

The detective checked her watch. "How about I take you with my partner? It's an unmarked car and will probably be better for you at the clinic as well."

"Thank you." September followed Detective Overton out of the building, a new lightness in her step. A weight she hadn't realized she'd been carrying stayed in the police station.

Thrive, not survive. She could do that.

DALLAS WEATHER WASN'T MUCH BETTER than Chicago's in late February, and they needed to wait for the plane to be deiced, delaying the flight. DFW airport was busier than O'Hare had been in the early morning hours, and September hoped her knit hat and sunglasses were enough to keep any fans who might be traveling from recognizing her.

The loudspeaker popped a couple times before a garbled voice announced boarding for her flight. Seated in first class, September wasted no time settling into her window seat. She opened an in-flight magazine knowing that if she didn't make eye contact with the boarding passengers, most of them would ignore her presence. The article on the top ten places to visit in Nashville brought back a flood of memories of her parents. Late-night tour buses, hotel rooms, and airplanes had all been part of her early life. She'd first sung on stage with them when she was four years old. Entertainment life was fun, but it wasn't the life she wanted for Harmony. She'd spent almost as much time during the last decade at home as she had on the road. When she hired a new manager, she'd make it clear she only wanted to travel a couple months out of the year.

Her phone vibrated. She had several texts she'd been ignoring, wanting to answer the ones from Adam and Melanie in person. The new one had a Dallas area code. She opened it.

—Arrest warrant issued. Two counts attempted homicide. Contacted Illinois police. He will stay in jail. Have a nice flight.

September opened Adam's texts but didn't bother reading what he had sent that day, assuming they were inquiries to where she was and what she was doing.

—Just boarded a plane in Dallas. Will be in Chicago at 6:30-ish. Pick me up, please? Arrest warrants issued for Sven.

She closed her phone and put it in airplane mode, then went back to studying the pictures in the article.

Soon they were flying above the clouds, the sunshine pouring in through her window reflecting the hope she felt in her soul.

The desk officer at the county police department confirmed the judge was out of town on holiday and would return Tuesday morning. Sven would not be arraigned until Tuesday afternoon at the earliest.

Adam fist pumped the air. Now if September would return his call. There was a possibility she'd gone into hiding. Or, as his father pointed out, she may have gone to Dallas. If September had trusted him enough, she would have taken him too.

He resisted sending another text and tried to focus on something else, a difficult task with Harmony sleeping. Out of boredom and a desire to be distracted, he decided to go through all the boxes in his bedroom closet his mother had been begging him to clear out for years. He turned on the music on his phone to drown out the voices and thoughts in his head. It worked until one of September's songs came on.

"Is it too late to know that I am wrong now that you are gone? Is it too late to tell my heart it's time for a brand-new start?"

She'd debuted the song about a month after he'd returned to Chicago. But like a coward, he had told himself she must've written it long before he'd broken her heart.

A text came in. She would be home soon.

He replied, not knowing if she would've already shut off her phone.

Now to get through the next few hours.

As soon as the plane taxied toward the gate, September turned her phone on and checked to see if Adam had replied.

Nothing.

The hope that had been so bright as she flew above the clouds withered to match the winter weather on the ground. Her phone vibrated. Then vibrated again and again. She'd forgotten that sometimes there was a lag after turning her cell back on. She only looked for a text from Adam.

—I'll be there.

With no luggage to drag behind her, September rushed through the airport and out of the secure area. Adam was leaning against a post, a half smile on his face. As she neared, he pulled his hand from behind his back to reveal a bouquet of red roses. When she got close enough, she jumped into his arms and held him in a hug. "I'm sorry I couldn't tell you before I left. I was afraid if I did, I wouldn't have the courage to go. And I couldn't have you hear what I needed to say."

Adam tightened his arms, then leaned down and took her lips in a classic airport kiss exchanged by lovers separated for weeks, not hours. Only after it ended did she worry about smartphone-wielding fans. But who cared if their kiss was posted on every social media sight? She wanted the world to know they were together.

Adam kept one arm around her. "Let's get out of here. I got a call from the police department where I left Sven. They received the warrant. And as soon as his arraignment tomorrow, they will turn Sven over to the Dallas Police Department. Apparently they did some searching and found other outstanding warrants for him, mostly disorderly conduct and all misdemeanors. However, one took place in a federal building in Washington State, so he has a felony warrant out as well."

Adam's arm around her felt like a shield to the news, and instead of berating herself again for allowing Sven into her life at all, she focused on the fact he would be out of it forever. When Adam opened the back door to a car-service vehicle, September threw him a questioning look.

He leaned close to her ear. "I knew we would want to talk, and this vehicle has a privacy screen between the passengers and the driver, which will come in handy because I can't kiss you while I'm driving you home myself."

Epilogue

One year later.

September stood in Dr. Brooks' office, Harmony balanced on her hip. She held out the invitation to the doctor. "I hope you can come to our Valentine's Day wedding. You've been such a help this last year."

"I'm honored. And I'm glad you're taking this next step."

"A year ago, marriage to Adam was a dream I hardly dared follow no matter how badly I wanted to. I probably made him wait twice as long as any other woman would have under the circumstances, but I needed to be sure my decision was not based on postpartum pregnancy hormones or a desperate attempt to escape my depression."

Dr. Brooks smiled. "I think, as we discovered these last few months, that you are stronger than you ever thought you were."

"At least I didn't have to go through a trial. It kept some things out of the public spotlight. I feel fully ready to start on a new path." Harmony wiggled down and toddled to the corner to play with the basket of toys Dr. Brooks kept in her office.

Dr. Brooks waved to a chair. September sat down.

The doctor held up a CD of September's newest album, *Returning*. "By the way, your newest song, "Dawning of Tomorrow," is a favorite of my PPD patients—both those in the hospital and those who don't require that level of care. So many of them are finding hope in it. I think knowing someone famous had PPD makes them feel less isolated. Some media and your fans may not have been kind to you these last few months, but you need to know you are making a real difference in mothers' lives all over the country since they aren't afraid to talk about PPD anymore. My colleagues across the country write to me to thank you."

"I am glad I found a way to use my story to help others." September looked over her shoulder to check on Harmony.

"You haven't asked, but with marriage next week, you have probably wondered. Yes, it is a possibility you could suffer from postpartum depression again. Your case was complicated with an abnormal amount of stress, though, and I would be surprised if you suffer PPD again to the extent you did this time. Don't let fear stop you from having children. Most women who suffer from PPD don't need a clinical stay. With a support system like the Hastings family and early intervention, I predict you can give Harmony a sibling if you wish. Remember, PPD can start even before delivery. I expect you to call me wherever you are in the world if you even suspect PPD, and we will work through it. You've grown to be an extraordinary mother, and I can't wait to watch the rest of your amazing life unfold."

September stood and gave the doctor a half hug. "Then I definitely expect to see you next week."

"I'll be there."

Adam watched his bride proceed awkwardly down the aisle. In her left hand she held her bouquet, her right hand reaching down to hold Harmony's little hand. Dressed in pink, from the silk flowers in her hair to her patent-leather shoes, his little chubby angel danced and hopped on the rose petals scattered about, her smile stolen from a mischievous cupid. September looked from Adam to his daughter—well, she would be legally next week. The corners of her lips twitched as if the serene bride smile she was trying to hold would slip any moment in a loud laugh.

Harmony pointed with the hand she dragged her pink giraffe in. "Da-dad!"

When September let go of Harmony's hand, the toddler careened up the aisle as fast as her plump legs could carry her. She tripped and fell but got up and found her balance and continued the race up the aisle. Muffled laughter filled the room. Adam squatted down and held out his arms.

"Da-dad!" Harmony flew into his arms.

Adam straightened and waited for his bride.

"Mama! Mama!" Harmony laughed and clapped as September completed her march, all traces of serenity gone in her wide smile.

When September reached his side, Harmony switched allegiance and dove for her mother, squashing September's bouquet in the process. Melanie, their matron of honor, hurried to extract both flowers and child from the situation. "Gam!" Harmony patted Melanie's cheeks as Melanie walked to the far side of the chapel.

Adam took September's hands in his, then turned and nodded at the minister. Happily ever after started now.

Dear Reader,

LIKE MANY MOTHERS, I EXPERIENCED PPD after the birth of each of my children. In writing September's story, I made the choice to focus on her bright moments rather than on the darkness of PPD. I realize some may criticize me for not showing enough of the pain, especially since I chose to have September find help in an in-patient facility. To be honest, I don't think I have the skills necessary to adequately take my reader through some of my darkest moments. I prefer to dwell on the hope that is at the end of the tunnel and knowing there is joy in motherhood and in the dawning of tomorrow.

More than the baby blues, postpartum depression and its cousin, postpartum psychosis, are best treated by professionals. If you or someone you love are overwhelmed by depression, please contact your health-care provider.

acknowledgements

THIS BOOK IS DEDICATED TO a reader I met through her reviews of my books. Months ago when Julie read *Mending Images with the Billionaire*, she asked if I would write Abbie's brother's stories . . . Well here they start. Thanks for the encouragement.

I also need to thank my friend Evan for rescuing me on my cover. Anna and Jon for the legal advice to jail Sven.

Thanks to Tammy and Nanette who are so willing to help make all my projects better and to read for all my mistakes. I would never make it through a day without Sally and Cindy whose advice keeps me going. Thank you wonderful ladies.

Michele at Eschler Editing does the best edits; any mistakes left in this book are not her fault. Nor are my excellent proofreaders to be blamed. Thank you ladies and gents!

My family, for sharing their home with the fictional characters who often got fed better than they did. And my husband who encourages me every crazy step of the way and puts up with all my messy spreadsheets.

And to my Father in Heaven for putting these wonderful people, and any I may have forgotten to mention, in my life. I am grateful for every experience and blessing I have been granted.

LORIN GRACE WAS BORN IN Colorado and has been moving around the country ever since, living in eight states and several imaginary worlds. She graduated from Brigham Young University with a degree in Graphic Design.

Currently she lives in northern Utah with her husband, four children, and a dog who is insanely jealous of her laptop. When not writing, Lorin enjoys creating graphics, visiting historical sites, museums, and reading.

Lorin is an active member of the League of Utah Writers and was awarded Honorable Mention in their 2016 creative writing contest short romance story category. Her debut novel, *Waking Lucy,* was awarded a 2017 Recommended Read award in the LUW Published book contest. In 2018 Mending Fences with the Billionaire, also received a Recommended Read award.

You can learn more about her, and sign up for her writers club at loringrace.com or at Facebook: LorinGraceWriter

Made in the USA
Monee, IL
29 July 2022